"Disappeared?"

"Yes. We cannot raise him on his interplantary transceiver and the Medean authorities cannot find him. They have concluded that he has met with foul play. At whose hands they cannot discover."

"But . . . but don't we have an embassy on that world?"

Mulk Jhabvola nodded. "A small one. They have been able to discover nothing. He is presumed dead."

Venu stared at his uncle. In spite of the other's efforts to look sympathetic, the satisfaction showed through.

MACK REYNOLDS

SPACE SEARCH

DELL / EMERALD

Published by
Dell Publishing Co., Inc.
1 Dag Hammarskjold Plaza
New York, New York 10017

Dell ® TM 681510, Dell Publishing Co., Inc.

ISBN: 0-440-08095-9

Printed in the United States of America

First printing—November 1984

Space Search

1

Perhaps Venu Jhabvola would have hesitated if he had been able to foresee the developments that would follow his departure from Harappa, the planet of his birth, to search for his father.

Venu had been surprised when, shortly before his 17th birthday, he was summoned to the presence of Khushwant Narayan, Guru of the University of New Bombay. He had never met the Brahman and had never expected to. As a member of the Vaishyas, he was fortunate enough to attend the upper caste school. He knew it was a concession to the high regard held for the sub-caste his father headed, that of the Expediters. It was widely believed that when and if there was an opening in the fifty families of Kshatriyas who ruled his world that the Expediters might well be picked to be raised to that degree, an event that had not taken place in Harappan history for more than a century.

He was accompanied by his sister, Santha, who was a year younger than Venu and a freshman. She had changed from student garb to a formal sari of green and gold, and had, for the unprecedented occasion, dabbed her forehead with a crimson caste mark. Venu himself had carefully bathed in the holy pool of the Mandar Temple, and wore a formal achkan—a high-necked tunic—over jodhpur breeches.

Santha was as bewildered by the summons as was he. They conferred briefly before heading for the university administration building, which was a replica of the Lakshmi Narayan Hindu Temple back on Earth from which their own planet had been settled centuries ago.

But neither could contribute anything. They had been simply instructed to repair to the offices of the guru.

Santha demurely following, as befitted a girl walking with her elder brother, they set out down the long, pool-flanked path to the garden-surrounded building of administration.

At the portal, with its lotus bundle columns and scalloped arches, rich with arabesques, they were met by a secretary, who gave them no more than greetings and led the way to the inner private office of Guru Khushwant Narayan.

They entered, side by side, and the secretary bowed slightly and withdrew, closing the door behind him.

Venu had often seen the university's guru on Tri-Di television but had never been this close before. The other, being a Brahman, was lighter of skin than either of the two students, and was seated behind a desk, the sacred thread of the Brahmans over one shoulder and the mark of Vishnu, The Preserver, chalked on his forehead, rising from the bridge of his nose like two thin white horns.

Both Venu and Santha blinked when they recognized their uncle, Mulk Jhabvola, seated next to the desk. His face was even tighter than usual but there was something else in his expression that Venu couldn't put his finger on. There was no love between them, the two students knowing full well that the heavy-set merchant resented the fact that Sudhin Jhabvola, their father, was rishi of the Expediters, rather than he. Mulk Jhabvola was above all ambitious, and from his youth his older brother had thwarted him.

Both Venu and Santha put their palms together and slightly out from their chests, bowed to the guru and said, in unison, "Namastey," and then turned to Mulk Jhabvola and repeated the Hindu universal formal greeting.

The guru, a handsome man in his middle years and, as a Brahman, with his Aryan heritage, somewhat taller than either Venu or Mulk, nodded to the newcomers, his face very serious.

"Be seated, my children," he said gently. "I am distressed that the occasion is one of bad tidings."

Venu froze slightly before taking the proffered chair. It could only be about his parent, who was off on a space expedition to another planet.

The guru said gently, "It is indicated that Rishi Sudhin Jhabvola, your father, has met disaster in the service of Harappa."

"Disaster!" Santha blurted. The three males ignored her. It was unseemly for a girl to speak in the presence of men without being directly addressed.

The guru turned to Mulk Jhabvola. "As the young people's uncle and acting rishi of your sub-caste, perhaps it would be best if you gave Venu and Santha the details."

The merchant's voice was unctuous. He said, "As you possibly know, your father, in his role as an Expediter, had journeyed to the planet Medea to arrange for an exchange of their uranium to the planet Basque in return for electronic equipment, so that the Basques in turn could trade the uranium to us, in return for star sapphires and other gems. Basque did not need the uranium itself, but had nothing, otherwise, of interest to us to trade. It was, in short, a three-way arrangement."

"But, uncle," Venu said, "what happened to father? Was it an accident in space? Did something happen to the spacecraft?"

The other shook his head. "No. He arrived safely on Medea. He even began the transactions, in competition with other interests also desiring the uranium trade. But suddenly he disappeared."

"Disappeared?"

"Yes. We cannot raise him on his interplanetary transceiver and the Medean authorities cannot find him. They have concluded that he has met with foul play. At whose hands they cannot discover."

"But . . . but don't we have an embassy on that world?"

Mulk Jhabvola nodded. "A small one. They have been able to discover nothing. He is presumed dead."

Venu stared at his uncle. In spite of the other's efforts to look sympathetic, the satisfaction showed through.

And why shouldn't it? It would be eight years before Venu would be of age. Eight years in which Mulk Jhabvola would be acting rishi of the family and of the Expediters' sub-caste. That would most certainly be sufficient time for him to entrench himself in the office to the point that even when Venu was of full manhood—twenty-five—he would never succeed to his father's rank. Competition for positions of power was strong on Harappa and ambitious men such as his uncle would resort to almost anything to dominate as potent a sub-caste as the Expediters, particularly in view of the fact that it was seemingly only a matter of time before the Vaishya sub-caste was raised to the Kshatriya caste, which exercised control of the government.

Venu said quickly, "I must go to Medea to find my father."

Santha said, "Yes!"

His uncle didn't bother to hide his impatience. He said, "Don't be ridiculous. You are but a lad, and besides, both our embassy and the Medean authorities have done their utmost to find Sudhin and have failed. He has disappeared completely. They cannot even get a cross on his transceiver with their communications computers. It has obviously been destroyed."

Venu was on his feet, his face and voice urgent. "I must go!"

Mulk Jhabvola said sternly. "As acting rishi of the Jhabvola family, I forbid you to further consider the matter. It is out of the question and you are being most unseemly."

The guru frowned slightly, but said nothing. Even though he was a Brahman, he did not feel it seemly to intervene. He could, of course, have overruled the lower-caste man, but in actuality he himself thought the desire of Venu unreasonable. He felt for the young man, but what was there to do?

The guru said, "Undoubtedly, my children, you will wish to return to your family estate for the ceremonies. I give you permission to take leave of the university for the required period."

Mulk Jhabvola said thoughtfully, "Perhaps not to return. I have never thought much of higher education for women, and as for you, Venu, I am not sure you are cut out for the scholarly life. Perhaps it would be more realistic for you to go immediately into the family business and learn expediting."

Venu was shocked. "But if I am one day to become rishi of the sub-caste, as my father before me, it is necessary that I have university schooling."

"I shall consider the matter further, following the funeral ceremonies," his uncle said condescendingly.

2

Venu and Santha, returning to their small bungalow in one of the student compounds, were aghast.

Santha said, "But what has Uncle Mulk in mind, brother? Surely you must attend the university. Already you have taken honors for three years and you are still but seventeen. As you told him, if ever you are to take the position of rishi, you must be the best educated male of our family."

Venu said bitterly, "If I am compelled to go down from the university, I have no doubt that shortly Uncle Mulk will make arrangements for our cousin, Bharata, to attend in our place. Bharata is brilliant enough and the son of his father. He would take every measure to secure enough prestige that when

the family elders voted upon the new rishi,
I would be deemed inadequate to take over
father's position, but Bharata would be
found to hold the qualifications. Undoubtedly, he would be but a figurehead for
Uncle Mulk for years to come."

"But Uncle Mulk is father's own brother!"

He could see she had little knowledge of
the men's world of angling for power, wealth,
and prestige. But then, as a girl, she had no
need to have. In due time, a suitable hus-
band would be found for her through family dickerings with acceptable other families
of their same caste level who had bachelor
sons. A suitable dowry would be paid, and
Santha would move to her new home to
take up the tasks of womanhood. So were
the traditions brought from Mother India,
long centuries past, and still followed on
this far world, on the rim of the sun sys-
tems settled by Earthlings.

"Yes," he said emptily, "Uncle Mulk is
father's brother." He didn't bother to mention the considerable difference between the
two men.

They reached the compound and made
their way through the garden walks to their
own bungalow, which they shared. A girl,
even though a student at the New Bombay
University, the most preeminent on Harappa,
could not be expected to live alone, without
supervision on the part of at least one male
member of her family.

To their surprise, when they entered, they found their two closest friends, the Gupta twins, Attia and Kamala, son and daughter of Chandra Gupta, most high in the politics of this province and of Harappa.

Kamala, sari clad as was Santha, but with the caste mark of the Kshatriyas on her forehead, came quickly to her feet from the divan upon which the two had been seated and hurried, with Indian grace, to take Santha in her arms.

Attia stood too. He was dressed as Venu, in achkan and jodhpurs. Obviously, the two of them had attired themselves for a formal occasion.

Attia put the palms of his hands together and bowed slightly to Venu and then to Santha. He said, expressionlessly, "Namastey, friends Venu and Santha. And . . . and condolences."

Venu returned the greeting. It was the first time in their years of relationship that his friend had ever saluted him in formality.

He said, "Then you have heard the news of our parent?"

Attia nodded, looking infinitely pained. "My father revealed the matter this morning."

Santha was weeping silently onto Kamala's shoulder.

The twins were Venu's age. They were intelligent of face, handsome of features. If it hadn't been for the fact that Kamala was

16

of higher caste and hence beyond him, Venu would have urged his father to begin the lengthy negotiations to make the girl his bride. But that, of course, could not be.

Venu said, "Please be seated, our good friends. It is typical of you to come to share our grief. Can I offer you a sherbet?"

Kamala seated herself next to Santha, her arm still around the other. Attia returned to his divan seat, less formal now.

He said, "We shall be present at the ceremonies, of course. Then, I assume, after a decent period of mourning, you will return to us here at the university."

Venu shook his head. "My Uncle Mulk is now acting rishi of our family, and, indeed, as such, acting rishi of the Expediters subcaste. His desires are our commands. Right before the guru, he informed us that he did not believe in higher education for women and that he didn't think me suitable for the scholarly life."

Kamala said, "But what do you mean, Venu? That is ridiculous."

"Please," Venu said, "You speak of my uncle and the acting head of my family."

Attia bit out, "He is trying to seize the position which is rightfully to be yours!"

Santha shook her head and said softly, "Venu wished to journey to this planet Medea and see if he could find trace of father, but Unle Mulk forbade him."

"Why?" Attia snapped.

Venu looked at him. "He said I was but a lad."

His friend came to his feet and paced the floor in mounting anger. "Yes, but a lad. However, if you were successful in the quest, your uncle would again be removed to a position of lesser honors. It is obvious that he does not wish your father to be found."

"Please," Venu said, as an honorable young man must, "you should not speak in my presence against the brother of my father. It is not seemly. Besides, the local authorites on Medea have been able to find no trace of Sudhin Jhabvola and he is presumed dead."

Attia's anger was growing. "Do not chide me, Venu Jhabvola. Pray remember that I am a Kshatriya and you but a Vaishya. Now come with me." He turned to the two girls. "We go to confer with my father, Gaewar of the Kshatriya caste of New Bombay."

Venu Jhabvola, aghast at his friend, protested all the way to the palace. However, Attia was having none of it. They took one of the new anti-gravity, automated rickshaws and Venu's upper-caste friend dialed their destination. It was one of the few times Venu had ever ridden on one of the ultra-modern means of local transportation, in spite of the fact that his father had expedited its import into Harappa from the planet Techno. There had been murmurings at the time, from the more traditional. Harappan elders, in particular, did not take kindly to new innovations. They had originally fled to this world to escape the break with hoary leftovers from yesteryear on Earth, and dragged their feet at each advance here on Harappa.

They entered the Gaewar's palace through a monstrous gate that reared itself a full hundred feet into the air, and then proceeded to the Keep.

They dismounted from their vehicle and ascended the stairs of the platform on which the inner palace was constructed. Upon their approach, two Sikh guards sprang to the salute, their ceremonial swords across their right shoulders. They were taller than the two students and burlier—professional soldiers and guards for twenty centuries and more. They wore the traditional thick beards, caught up in a little net, and orange turbans about their heads. Venu knew that by their religious laws, somewhat different from the Hindu, they never shaved nor cut their hair, and it was deemed a great insult for them ever to be seen, by other than their immediate family, with their turbans off. They were also supposed to wear a wooden comb in their hair, an iron bangle on a wrist, and to carry an iron-handled knife. All of these customs went far back into the mists of antiquity.

Attia didn't bother to acknowledge the salute in any manner, but led the way on into the Keep. Venu had on occasion visited the Gupta twins in their home, here in the palace grounds, but that had been the family quarters, never the Keep where the official business of New Bombay province was conducted. On the outside, it seemed a medieval Indian construction, but deep beneath the planet were extensive offices, long halls, and chambers, complete with computers, data files, and the rest of the automated-computerized equipment of modern technology. Harappa seemed old only on the surface.

They halted, finally, in a large, magnificently done reception room, well packed with those soliciting the attention of the powerful man within. A secretary scurried up to them. He greeted Attia with palms together, as though praying, and the usual "Namastey" greeting as he bobbed bows. After all, Attia was the only son of the Gaewar and might well one day take his father's place as one of the most influential men on Harappa.

Attia said curtly, "Is my father free?" Although he was of the ruling caste himself, he disliked overly subservient underlings. It was a sign of his being one of the up-and-coming generation that he had chosen Venu, of a lower caste, to become his best friend. Attia Gupta was no class snob.

The other bowed slightly again. "He is in conference, but should be free very shortly. It is to be assumed that it is a matter of importance?"

Attia looked at him. "Do you imagine I would intrude upon the Gaewar, while he is holding audiences, if it were otherwise?"

The other bowed again, nervously, and indicated chairs for the two.

Attia growled to Venu, after the secretary had left to announce them, "The more they crawl on their bellies to you, the more they hate you. If I were a high-ranking official, I would surround myself with men willing to argue with me when they disagreed with my opinions."

Venu looked at him from the side of his eyes, and for the first time since he had heard of his father's disappearance allowed an edge of humor. "We shall see about that when they have elevated you to Gaewar, my friend."

They were shortly ushered into the inner office where Chandra Gupta held forth. As lavish as the outer rooms of the Keep had been, the ultimate room of the Gaewar was spartan in furniture and decoration, as was its occupant in dress. The Gaewar had not been the first ruler in history to learn to gain prestige by avoiding ostentation before his underlings, many of whom attired and bejeweled themselves considerably more richly than did he. He wore a simple uniform in a land that did not tend to simplicity in costume and he bore himself with a soldier's posture. His face was tired, but strict, and he was obviously one given to command.

The Gaewar looked at his son questioningly, after the amenities of greetings and introduction had been dispensed with. Venu had never met his close friend's illustrious parent before, any more than he had met the guru of the university, and, so far were they above him, he had never expected to.

Chandra Gupta must have realized that something extraordinary was in the wind. His son was not that undisciplined as to break in upon so busy a man without cause. However, the Gaewar held his peace and merely nodded to his offspring.

Attia said strongly, "I come in behalf of my friend, Venu Jhabvola, son of Rishi Sudhin Jhabvola, of the Expediters subcaste."

The Gaewar looked at Venu and nodded. "I knew your father and valued him, my son. He was a competent and honorable man." He hesitated and then said, "I have heard the news. I offer my condolences. Please sit down, young gentlemen."

The students sat and the Gaewar looked at his son. "Please elucidate. Why should it be necessary for you to intervene on behalf of Venu Jhabvola?"

Attia went through the story quickly but well. When he was finished he lapsed into the same silence Venu held, waiting for his father's word.

Chandra Gupta thought about it. He stared off into a far corner of the room. "There is another element to it," he said finally.

The younger men looked at him.

He said, "It is a seldom-evoked tradition, since there is so seldom a need for utilizing it. As I recall, the report from Medea is that Rishi Jhabvola has disappeared. There is no evidence of how, or why."

Venu said, "Yes, Bahadur," using the salutation of respect.

"Then no body has been produced as evidence that he is dead?"

"No, Bahadur."

The Gaewar put the tips of his fingers together and leaned back in his chair. "By our traditions, if a rishi dies of natural causes or by accident, and his eldest son is not of age twenty-five, then a brother, or other relative if there is no brother, becomes acting rishi until the son is of age. At that time, the elders of the family gather. If it is deemed that the eldest son is competent to hold down the office, he becomes rishi. If the elders determine that he is not competent, then they search among the other men of the hereditary ruling family of the caste or sub-caste and try to find one who is suitable."

Venu wondered why this recapitulation of a fact of Harappan society known to even a ten-year-old was necessary. He said, politely, "Yes, Bahadur." But his expression must have shown he was mystified.

The Gaewar nodded. "However, I mention the seldom invoked tradition. If a rishi dies of violence by the hand of another, then his son, even though not of age, succeeds to the rank. It is most usual that the elders select advisers to assist him until he is of age, but he is officially rishi."

Venu looked at him blankly. "I did not know of this, Bahadur."

"Few people do," Chandra Gupta said.

"But, Father, that means . . ." Attia blurted.

"Silence a moment, my son," his parent said. He looked back at Venu. "The reason is this. Unscrupulous men are sometimes so dishonorable as to seek the death of a rishi so that they can usurp his rank, particularly if his eldest son is underage. This tradition insures that it is impractical to assassinate the head of a family, or sub-caste, or caste. Nothing is gained."

Attia said urgently, "Sire, that means if Venu can prove that his father Sudhin died by violence, then he is immediately appointed rishi."

Venu said in puzzlement, "But my father died on a far world. If it was by personal violence, then it was on the part of otherworldlings, not a person of Harappa."

The Gaewar shook his head. "It makes no difference, son of my friend. By our tradition, if your father has died of personal violence, you are rishi of your family. You see, by such custom it makes it impractical for a villain to hire the services of another to commit his deed of violence. If Sudhin Jhabvola can be proven to have died of personal violence, you are rishi of the Jhabvola family and hence of the Expediters sub-caste."

He turned to his auto-secretary and activated it. He said, "This by the command of the Gaewar, Venu Jhabvola, son of Sudhin Jhabvola, is ordered to repair to the planet Medea to investigate the circumstances of the disappearance of his father. It is instructed that acting rishi Mulk Jhabvola issue him sufficient interplanetary credits to finance his travels to and from Medea."

He flicked another switch and said, "This order is to be issued to Mulk Jhabvola immediately."

He turned back to the two students. "And now, my sons, I am very busy."

3

At the evening meal that day, Venu sat with Mulk Jhabvola and the other older male members of the immediate family. Santha, of course, would eat later with the women and younger children.

Venu kept his eyes to his food, knowing that his uncle was incensed. Incensed, but incapable of reacting against the order of the Gaewar.

Venu took up a small amount of rice from the thali, the large metal plate before him, and deftly rolled it into a snowball before dipping it into one of the small katorie bowls surrounding the plate. That particular katorie contained mint curry, one of his favorites. He popped the rice expertly into his mouth and reached for more, his eyes still low.

His uncle said, making little effort to keep anger from his voice, "So you saw fit to approach the Gaewar, in spite of my instructions to refrain from considering further this fantastic wild goose chase to Medea!"

"No, Uncle," Venu said slowly. "It was suggested by Attia Gupta to attend upon his father. Attia is a Kshatriya, hence it was unseemly not to conform to his wishes."

"Unseemly, perhaps," his uncle snorted, "but not impossible, by our usage. Without doubt, you made a great show of yourself before the Gaewar, revealing the innermost affairs of our family."

"No, Uncle. The Gaewar was already aware of the disappearance of my father."

"And you talked him into issuing this ridiculous order to provide you with sufficient interplanetary credits to journey to and from Medea!"

Venu did his utmost to keep inflection from his own voice. After all, this man was acting rishi of the family and hence due great respect. He said, carefully, "No, Uncle. I spoke very little at all in the Gaewar's presence. I was surprised when, on his own initiative, he issued the order. He did not consult with me."

All of which was true, of course, though

Venu was somewhat stretching the point. He most certainly had not protested the command.

He must, he decided, be a man among men, not a shrinking lad. He brought his eyes up and looked into his uncle's. The other men at the table continued eating, possibly somewhat hurriedly, and kept their peace. They were new to the fact that the largely unpopular Mulk was now acting rishi of the family, rather than the quiet, gentle, and well-loved Sudhin.

Mulk Jhabvola was furious. Had not his complexion already been so dark, a deep flush would have been evident.

He snapped, "Very well. An order from the Gaewar must be heeded, no matter how poorly advised he might have been in issuing it. However, pray note, beloved nephew, that the order states that sufficient interplanetary credits be issued to finance your travels to and from Medca. Nothing is said about your expenses upon Medea itself."

Venu stared at him blankly. He said, "But Uncle, how can I survive on an alien planet without resources?"

"The problem is not mine," the other said bluntly. He turned to Bharata, his own son, a slight boy of eighteen, who sat on his father's right, a snide quirk of amusement on his lips. "Tomorrow we will take measures to insure your entry into the University of New Bombay. Undoubtedly, in view of my present position as rishi of the Expediters sub-caste, you will be accepted."

Venu could only note that his uncle had said rishi, not acting rishi.

4

At the spaceport, where Santha, Attia and Kamala had accompanied him to see him off, Venu told them of his dilemma.

Santha simply stared at him.

Attia said, "But this is ridiculous. We'll return to my father and have him order Mulk Jhabvola to supply you with sufficient funds to cover your expenses on Medea."

But Venu shook his head. "No. Already my uncle is greatly angered by my seeing the Gaewar. If I returned and a new order was issued him, he would be infuriated beyond belief."

"Let him be infuriated!" Attia said indignantly.

Venu looked at his friend. "Pray remember that not only I but Santha will most likely be under my uncle's domination for the rest of our lives. What sort of a dowry will he allow her from the family resources if I continue to thwart him? What sort of a position will he appoint me to in the Expediters sub-caste? Our lives are in his hands, Attia."

"But what can you do?"

A steel ladder was descending from the spaceship and others standing on the spaceport tarmac began heading for the saucer-shaped vessel.

"I don't know," Venu said. "Never before in my life have I been in a spacecraft. Indeed, I have never been out of the province of New Bombay, not to speak of being on another world. I do not even know what language they speak on Medea."

Attia said gruffly, "I understand that just about anywhere in the Allied Worlds confederation they speak Amer-English as a second language if not a first, just as we do. It has become the interplanetary lingua franca."

"I must go," Venu said. He turned to his sister, who was blinking to hold back tears, took her by the shoulders and kissed her fondly on the forehead. "While I am gone . . ." He took a deep breath and shook his head. "No, there is nothing I can say. You must now obey the orders of the acting rishi, and of the women of his family, since both

31

our mother and father are now gone and we have no home of our own. And you must do your duties as you have been so well trained to do them while in the household of our father."

He turned to Attia and they shook hands clumsily. To Kamala he bowed and smiled, since on Harappa, a male of other than her own family does not touch a girl who has reached puberty.

He turned and hurried toward the spaceship.

5

The Spaceship *Hammerfest IV* was out of New Bergen, a planet so lacking in natural resources that the inhabitants largely resorted to interplanetary commerce to accrue sufficient credits to allow for the import of their necessities. New Bergen was not alone in this field of endeavor, though it had a comparative monopoly in this sector of the galaxy. Among the 5,000 planets Earth had settled, many had insufficient interplanetary commerce or passengers to allow for a spacefleet, even had they wished one, which many didn't.

Harappa, though not particularly isolationist, was among those worlds that, at least until recently, had seldom had occasion for trade of any magnitude. Seldom did her people desire to travel, save for pilgrimages to Earth and to Mother India. Individuals seldom repeated a trip even there. India was no longer the same place it had been when it had sent forth the colonists to Harappa. The institutions that the Harappans had taken with them were no longer to be found. Famed temples, replicas of which were still devoutly utilized in the colony world, were now museums on a cynical, ultra-advanced Earth. Customs still followed on the daughter world were only read about in anthropology classes on the mother world. Political institutions on the home planet were unrecognizable on conservative Harappa. It could prove traumatic to the nostalgic tourist from the still-Hindu world out on the rim of Allied Worlds.

So it was that until recently Harappa had not developed a spacefleet, but relied largely on the carriers of other planets to provide her with cargo and passenger services to the extent she needed them. Times were changing, somewhat, explaining the rapid growth of the Expediters sub-caste that was accelerating Harappan trade, often despite the anguish of the more conservative elements.

As a result of the efforts of such as Sudhin Jhabvola, Harappa was being dragged into the present and future, in spite of itself. In the near future, undoubtedly, it would secure the technology to build its own fleet of spacecraft.

The SS *Hammerfest IV* was basically a cargo craft, making semi-regular stops at the half dozen worlds it covered each year. However, its schedule was often revised if a particularly large cargo was available to be carted from one planet to another. Hence, it was not dependable for passenger services, if one were shipping through to a planet several stops beyond Harappa.

Ordinarily, Venu Jhabvola would have waited until a more tightly scheduled passenger craft had descended upon the New Bombay spaceport, but he was in a great hurry, so he took the first vessel that offered him passage to Medea. He was the only passenger aboard.

Venu Jhabvola concentrated on learning what he could of the planet Medea while on the ship. He had heard practically nothing on Harappa, beyond the fact that Medea was rich in radioactive elements and was hence able to earn considerable interplanetary credits from worlds less richly endowed, such as Harappa, whose newly booming nuclear power centers were desperate in their need for uranium.

The *Hammerfest* crewed two "deck" officers, the captain, Nils Anderson, and his mate; two engineers, the chief and his assistant; a chief steward and his second steward. Their time was spent largely in idleness, but they were on hand.

In spite of his youth, Venu Jhabvola was well received by them all. This was the first time they had picked up a passenger from Harappa. All of them had been on a score of worlds, but they knew little of Harappa and its institutions and had a thousand questions to ask Venu.

Venu, in turn, knew little about other Earthling-populated worlds. When there are 5,000 of these, the merest smattering about each of them is beyond even a keen student, unless his major is in interplanetary affairs. That was not Venu's field, although as a member of the Expediters sub-caste he would very likely travel interspace, as had his father.

His favorite among the crew was the first officer, who was the ship's navigator and second in command. He was a tall, blond man in the Norwegian tradition, blue of eye and handsome in a craggy sort of way. As a physical specimen, he was about as far as one could get from the slight and delicately featured Harappan, but he was friendly and probably the most intelligent man on the ship.

They played battle chess for long hours, their conversation covering every field in which they were both interested. Although discussing any world that First Officer

Kristian Tryggvason had visited was fascinating for Venu, he was particularly interested in Medea.

It was, Kristian Tryggvason informed him, a planet belonging to a sun system that had but one other inhabited world, Tangier. For Kris's money, Tangier was by far the more interesting of the two. He considered Medea to be on the grim side.

"In what way?" Venu asked, carefully advancing one of his tanks across the battle chess board. On Harappa, battle chess was so ardently played that they taught it in school and gave credits. However, the first officer had been forced to play the game so much to relieve spaceship tedium that they were a fairly equal match.

Tryggvason shrugged. "Technology. I don't mind developing industry, science, industrial techniques that in the long run save labor, but I don't want to eat, drink, and sleep technology. What their ultimate goal is, I don't know, and I doubt if they do, but they're heading for it under forced draft. I get tired just watching them."

Venu frowned. "But surely they must take time to contemplate, to meditate, to commune with the gods—Brahma, the Creator, Vishnu the Preserver, Siva the Destroyer."

Kris laughed and covered the advance of Venu's tank by moving one of his fortresses.

He said, "If they had a god, they'd mechanize him."

Venu said in dismay, "One must not speak lightly of a god."

Kris said, "There are gods and gods, I've found. Some of them deserve to be spoken lightly of."

Venu said stiffly, "We Hindus say God is one. People just call him by different names."

"You just mentioned the gods, not god. Brahma, Vishnu, and what was the other one?"

"Siva, the Destroyer. But the three are in actuality but manifestations of the one god. You see . . ."

But the Norwegian shook his head. "Don't try to tell me. I'll just get a headache. But answer me this. A few centuries ago a colonizing ship, heading out to find a new world, crashed. The one big requirement to join this expedition was that each colonist have an I.Q. of at least 150. They figured on developing a world of super-intellects—geniuses. However, through some malfunction of their ship, it dropped out of hyperspace and cracked up on a planet far, far from the nearest Allied Worlds member. A space patrol found them recently. The crash had turned them back into a primitive society, since they had lost all of their machinery, for all practical purposes, and most of their books. So what kind of a god had evolved? Tonatiuh, the sun god of the Aztecs."

"Tonatiuh?" Venu said questioningly, bringing up another tank in an attempt to flank his opponent.

"Yes. Evidently one of the few books that had survived was on the mythology of Ancient Mexico. Tonatiuh required blood sacrifices, in which the heart was torn from the chest of the victim after the chest had been sliced open with a ceremonial knife." The first officer finished grimly. "It was quite a religion. Can you identify Tonatiuh with your one god in his many manifestations?"

Venu was upset. All Harappans were either Hindu or Sikh, a related religion. He had never argued religion with someone of another faith. He had known that there *were* other faiths, but he had never discussed them, or even read about them, save in books written by Harappans, who were, obviously, somewhat prejudiced in favor of their own religion.

"By the sacred fire, Agni," Venu said. "Tonatiuh would seem to be a manifestation of the god Siva. He is a terrible god of destruction. He controls war, pestilence, famine, death, and related calamities like floods and droughts. Therefore, in the past, he had to be propitiated with praise and sacrifice. Siva, though he is most feared by human beings whose fortunes he can control, is condemned to be a wanderer throughout time.

"Or perhaps this Tonatiuh is Siva's consort, Parvati, the most powerful goddess in the entire Hindu pantheon. When in a benevolent form she can be seen as a beautiful woman or loving wife, but she can also be Durga, goddess of battle, holding weapons of retribution in her ten hands. When she becomes Kali, the terrible black goddess who has conquered time, she wears a garland of skulls, her red tongue hangs out thirstily, and she must be propitiated by sacrifices."

The first officer was staring at him. "You believe all that, Venu?"

"But, of course," Venu said blankly. "I am a Hindu."

"And you believe in sacrificing to this Kali, or whatever her name was?"

Venu smiled ruefully, and looked down to cover his embarrassment. "You see, we no longer fear Siva or his consort on Harappa. Long past we have solved the evils of life. Even the Harijans live in plenty, and . . ."

"What is a Harijan?"

"An Outcaste, a person who has no caste. There are four castes—the Brahmans, who are priests and scholars, the Kshatriyas, who were warriors and rulers originally, the Vaishyas, my own caste, who are merchants and bankers, and the Sudras, originally peasants and artisans."

"And these Untouchables?"

"The Harijans are the Children of God, as the great guru Mahatma Gandhi called them when he freed them from their position of bondage, long years hence back in Mother India. In the past they were consigned only to the menial positions."

"Well, let's go back to this Siva who demands sacrifices. I had no idea that any such institutions still existed on Harappa."

Venu's smile was rueful again, even as he advanced his second tank through the ranks of the foot soldiers.

He said, "We have no wars, these days. Nor famines, nor pestilence, nor the other evils once presided over by Siva and Parvati. But even in the old days, before we colonized Harappa, the Hindus in Mother India no longer resorted to the blood sacrifices that prevailed in primitive times. The sacrifices consisted of flowers."

Kris saw that Venu's advance was threatening his field marshal piece and could lead to a checkmate. He hurriedly moved, even as he shook his head at the Harappan.

"Man is at his damnedest when he confronts his gods."

Venu looked at him. "Who said that?" he asked, pressing his attack by advancing a machinegun nest.

41

"I did," the first officer said, studying his position anxiously. "What was this about no more war? Don't you have any armies on your planet?"

"No, nor have we ever had. We follow the ahimsa doctrine of the Jain-Buddhist, that of non-violence. We have world government." Venu's eyes had also narrowed over the now close-fought game.

"Buddhist?" Kris Tryggvason said. "I'm not particularly up on comparative religion, but I thought Hinduism and Buddhism were two different religions." He brought one of his machinegun nests up to cover his field marshal.

Venu advanced his flanking tank still further, and said, "The Buddha was one of the reincarnations of Vishnu, the Preserver. But could we return, friend Kris, to the planet Medea and why you find it dull?"

The first officer was scowling at his position. If he didn't look out, it was going to be the third time in a row he had lost to this boy half his age.

He said, "It was settled by a contingent of Technocrats who were disgusted at the socioeconomic system that prevailed on Earth at that time."

"Technocrats?"

"An early organization first founded in what was then the United States in the 20th Century, I think. They were against the prevailing socioeconomic system, which was then called, sometimes laughingly, free enterprise. All of the means of production, communication, transportation, and distribution were privately owned."

"They were?" Venu said in surprise.

"Ummm." Kris brought up another of his foot soldiers.

"The Technocrats were of the opinion that the means of production should be managed by technicians, not by private individuals. They didn't get very far and, after hyperspace had been found and interstar flights became practical, they banded together in disgust and decided to seek out a world of their own where they could go to hell in their own way."

"Hell?" Venu said. He moved the tank again and added, "Check."

"Hell," the first officer said. "The place where sinners go when they die." He retired his field marshal behind one of his fortresses. He was on the run.

Venu stared at him. "But surely, if one errs in his present incarnation, in his next he but becomes a lower form of life, such as an insect, and has thus postponed his achievement of Nirvana until he can again acquire merit." He moved his first tank up another space and said again, "Check, ah, let me see. Yes, checkmate."

"Don't be ridiculous." The other stared at

43

the board. "You mean, you Hindus don't have a heaven and hell?"

"I have never heard of them, friend Kris. And it is quite difinitely checkmate. Your field marshal has no place to go."

"For somebody who claims his planet doesn't know war, you certainly do fight a good battle of battle chess," Kris Tryggvason grumbled.

6

Hour followed hour in their seemingly motionless progress through hyperspace. Venu fitted into the ship's routine so much so that he was surprised when Captain Anderson informed him that they were about to emerge into space proper, in preparation to land on Medea.

He approached the first officer and said, hiding his embarrassment, "Do I understand that when the *Hammerfest* lands it becomes necessary for you to enter the city, near the spaceport, to present certain papers to the authorities?"

"Why, yes," Kris said. "Either I or the captain, and he usually hands me that chore. We have to clear quarantine, customs, immigration, interplanetary pest control, that sort of red tape. Then we have to present our flight plan for our next destination."

"I . . . would it be possible for you to allow me to go with you? That is, into the city?"

"Why not, if you wish? But there will be public transportation at the terminal. As I recall, Medea has the same type of anti-gravity vehicles as you have on Harappa."

Venu said unhappily, "Unfortunately, I have no interplanetary credits with which to hire a vehicle."

Kris Tryggvason scowled at him. "No interplanetary credits? But it's not inexpensive to travel from Harappa to Medea. I thought you were rich."

"No," Venu said, attempting to keep bitterness from his voice. "I am no longer rich."

"Where did you want to go, to some hotel? Frankly, Venu, Medea is a strictly cash-on-the-barrelhead planet. If you don't have interplanetary credits . . ." He let the sentence dribble away.

"To the Harappan Embassy," Venu said. "Perhaps I can finish my business and be ready to depart by the time a new spacecraft leaves to return to Harappa."

"There isn't as much traffic between Medea and Harappa as all that," the first officer said. "You might have quite a wait. But I'll take you to the embassy. I don't know where it is, but it's undoubtedly in the vicinity of the Interplanetary Trade Building where I'll be headed. Most of the other planet embassies are."

When they had sat down on the Medean spaceport tarmac, Venu made his goodbyes to Captain Anderson and the others. To his surprise, the chief steward gave him a large plastic wicker hamper.

"A little snack," the steward said huskily. "In memory of the *Hammerfest*."

Venu was embarrassed. Undoubtedly, Kris Tryggvason had informed the other of Venu's lack of credits. But there was nothing he could do to salve his pride. He took the hamper, finding it quite heavy, and thanked the well-intentioned man formally. He could hardly inform the other that a Harrapan of good family did not accept gifts that could not be reciprocated. But perhaps someday the *Hammerfest* would return to Harappa and he would have the opportunity to present the chief steward with a seemly remembrance of Venu's home planet, such as a star sapphire.

Kris Tryggvason summoned an anti-gravity car on his pocket transceiver and he and Venu got into the vehicle after depositing the Harappan's luggage on the back seat. Their first stop was the administration building of the spaceport, where Kris saw them quickly through customs and immigration. As a bearer of an Allied Worlds Interplanetary Passport, Venu Jhabvola had no difficulties.

The immigration officer, who was dressed in the somewhat drab latest styles from Earth that were most often utilized through Allied Worlds, took Venu's Harappan attire in curiously but said only, "How long do you plan to be on Medea?"

"I . . . I don't know. Only long enough to . . . to transact some business."

"You seem rather young to be on a business trip. What is the nature of your business, please?"

"I seek my father, Sudhin Jhabvola."

"I see. I have heard of the case, on the Tri-Di news broadcasts. It created quite a stir. We don't have much of that sort of thing on Medea. Good luck, young man."

Venu bowed formally, "Thank you, sir."

The other stamped the passport and returned it.

Kris said, "Okay, let's get going."

The automated taxi sped them into the city after Kris had said into its screen, simply, "Harappan Embassy."

Venu was shocked by the Medean countryside. Used to the colorful buildings of his own world, the beautiful temples, the pagodas, the palaces, the parks and gardens, it was unbelievable that another people would actually permit ugly industrial plants to exist *above the surface*. Why, even heavily laden industrial trucks were plodding along the main highway, dominating the traffic. Had it never occurred to these technocrats to hide such unsightliness under the surface? The surface of a world, surely, was for man and the animals, birds and vegetation—not for the machine.

Kris looked at him from the side of his eyes and grinned. He said, "I told you it was a grim world. But you'd be surprised how much grimmer some of the others are."

"But it is so *ugly*. Why, everybody seems even to dress all but the same. And so colorlessly!"

"Possibly the price of affluence," Kris said. "They're so busy getting rich that they don't have time for art. And wait until you eat what they call food on this planet."

But then he must have remembered what Venu had told him about not having the wherewithal to buy anything on Medea. He said, "Look, boy, possibly you'll be able to get a job at the embassy to tide you over while you go about trying to find your father."

Venu shook his head. "I inquired into that before I left Harappa. All hiring by Harappan missions is done on Harappa before the mission leaves."

The first officer was unhappy. "Well, you won't find employment anywhere else. I understand that by Medea law aliens can't work on this planet. You're lucky that immigration officer didn't ask you about your resources. He never would have let you in. He must have automatically assumed, as I did, that the very fact that you are able to travel through space indicated you were in good funds. I don't know what in the devil you're going to do."

"Neither do I," Venu said miserably.

They were in the city now and, if anything, the efficient drabness increased, as did the traffic. Why, it must *all* be on the surface, Venu decided.

The Harappan embassy was a small one and housed in a building with a score of others. It was a colorless office with no charm whatsoever.

The hovercab pulled up at the curb. Its screen said, "The Harappan Embassy. Third floor."

"Here you are," Kris Tryggvason said uncomfortably. "Good luck, Venu." He remained in his seat while Venu got his two bags and the hamper of food the chief steward had given him from the back.

Venu put the things down on the sidewalk and put out his hand to shake farewell. "A thousand thanks, and may Lord Krishna see to your well being."

The first officer said, "Perhaps some day we'll see each other again, back on Harappa," as he shook.

"Who can say what paths Brahma, in his wisdom, will lead us down in this incarnation?" Venu returned formally.

He stood and watched after the cab for a moment when it had departed in the direction of the Interplanetary Trade Building.

He then took up his bags and hamper and mounted the steps of the building. The lobby was filled with hurrying men and women, the men dressed all but identically, the women almost so. Even when there was a touch of color in their costume, Venu noted, it was far from the bright textiles of his home world. Already the Harappan youth was becoming homesick for that with which he was familiar.

Elevators were little different than in New Bombay, he found, crowding into one whose arrow indicated it was heading upward. Some of his fellow passengers stared at his off-world attire, quite rudely he thought, but no one spoke. The door closed and they began to ascend. The compartment's screen called each floor and he got out at three.

There were signs facing the elevator bank, indicating the various offices on that floor. The Harappan Embassy was to the right.

He entered the small reception room and put down his things. The sole occupant of the office sat behind a desk to the room's far side. She was the first person of dark complexion Venu Jhabvola had seen since he had left his home world. Undoubtedly she was a Harappan, although she wore similar dress to that of the women of Medea. How she must long for a sari, Venu though irrelevantly.

He put the palms of his hands together, pointed upward, bowed and said, "Namastey."

"Good afternoon," she said briskly. She had no caste mark, of course, but undoubtedly in view of her position, she was a Vaishya like himself.

He said, "I am Venu Jhabvola, son of Rishi Sudhin Jhabvola, and I have come from Harappa to seek my father."

She blinked at that.

He said, "Whom would it be proper for me to see?"

"Why, I suppose Rana Kumbha, Secretary of the Interplanetary Trade Commission. It was he who worked with Rishi Jhabvola when your father was here."

"Then may I attend him, please?"

She did the things receptionists have done universally down through the ages, then looked up from her order box and said, "Rana Kumbha will see you immediately. The Interplanetary Trade Commission office is through that door and at the end of the hall."

Venu followed her directions, after asking if he could leave his things in the corner of the room. He decided, as he progressed down the short hallway, that the Harappan embassy on Medea was indeed small. He doubted if it consisted of as many as six persons.

There was what resembled a small TV screen set into the door lettered Interplanetary Trade Commission. It picked him up and the door opened automatically at his approach. The device was new to him. Harappa avoided utilizing gadgets that could be dispensed with, particularly if they jarred with aesthetics. Harappans would rather walk than ride, would rather sleep with woolen blankets over them than in an electrically warmed bed, would rather eat organic fruits and vegetables than synthetic ones, and were contemptuous of such devices as electric knives or toothbrushes.

The door swung open and Venu entered the tiny office beyond. There was one desk, several metal files, a voco-typer and other office equipment, and three chairs.

The occupant was standing. He was a stocky man beginning to push his middle years, so dark as to be a Dravidian, Venu decided, and he wore a mustache in the style of the city of Kula, Harappa's second largest. He, as the girl in the reception room, wore Medean clothing and looked uncomfortable in it. Small wonder, Venu thought.

Putting his hands together, the tips near

his chin in correct manner, he said, "Namastey, son of the former Rishi Jhabvola."

Venu returned the salute and said, "Namastey," as well.

"Please be seated. I am Rana Kumbha."

Venu seated himself and said, "I seek my father."

"So the receptionist has told me." The other shook his head regretfully, sadly, but definitely. "Then your cause is a lost one, Venu Jhabvola."

"If so, then I seek vengeance."

The other looked at him for a long moment, then sighed. He said, "I worked with your father, the rishni, on more than one occasion, on both this and other worlds. I respected him. However, he is no longer with us. May the gods will his reincarnation on a higher plane, in his path to Nirvana."

"When comes the wind and whither goes it?" Venu quoted correctly to the other's politeness. "But how can you be so sure that my father is dead? Perhaps he is a captive."

"If so, not upon Medea, Venu Jhabvola."

"How can you be positive of that?"

"Look at your passport, Venu Jhabvola."

Frowning, Venu took his interplanetary passport from the inner pocket of his achkan tunic, mystified.

The other said, "Look at the stamp the immigration officer put in it. It is of a special radioactive ink, with an identity number that applies only to you. The Medean police authorities have you on their direct-finder computers at all times. They know to within a square foot of where you are. If you left it somewhere, even by mistake, they would expel you from Medea. If you die, the radioactive element dies with you. Otherwise, the computers have a cross on you so long as you are on Medea. Besides that, your father had, of course, his personal transceiver. It is impossible to carry on ordinary day-by-day activities without it, since it is his interplanetary credit card as well as a means of communication. He could not eat, find lodging, transport himself, or buy either an object or a service without it. And the computers keep a cross on it as well. When your father, ah, disappeared, both crosses were lost."

Venu said desperately, "Perhaps he left the planet."

"If so, how? You must realize, Venu Jhabvola, that there is but one spaceport on Medea, the one where you landed. Medean authorities are most competent. Everything is most efficient on this world, to the point where it drives easy-going Harappans like us to despair. Your father could not have left Medea without them knowing."

Venu closed his eyes. "What happened on the day of his disappearance?" he asked softly.

The other shook his head. "We don't know. At one time he was at his hotel, preparing to making final arrangements for the trade of uranium to the planet Basque so that, in turn, they could trade it to us. He left the hotel for the appointment and was never seen again. Both his passport identification and that of his transceiver simply cut off, and the computers lost their cross on him."

Venu said slowly, "On Harappa, they mentioned the fact that there were others dickering for Medea's uranium."

"Yes, several. The most progressive planets of Allied Worlds utilize uranium but it is not present on many of them to any extent. Medea has more than ample for its own needs, but not an unlimited supply. Harappa wished to corner its entire export allotment. So did other worlds."

Venu said, "And when father was eliminated from the negotiating, who acquired the contract?"

"The planet Linus, whose agent was Hari Maroon. I assume you have heard of him?"

"No. Who is Hari Maroon, of the planet Linus?"

"He is not a citizen of Linus. He is a well-known free-lance, interplanetary trader."

"What is his home planet?"

Rana Kumbha shook his head again. "I do not know. Nor does there seem to be any record. Perhaps he has none."

"But everyone must have a home planet," Venu said, frowning his puzzlement.

"Not necessarily. Some worlds have strange rulings. On Monet, for instance, if two other-world citizens have a child, it is not a Monet citizen. And if a child comes from a world that does not accept citizenship of an infant not born on that world, then the child is worldless. If I am not mistaken, that is the status of Hari Maroon. He is somewhat of a notorious personage, though very wealthy."

"I see. And where would I find this Hari Maroon, who seems to be the only person who has profited by my father's disappearance?"

"I wouldn't know. Upon achieving the contract for his patrons on Linus, he left this planet."

Venu was in despair. "How could I possibly locate him? Obviously, he must be questioned. He alone has gained."

The other said sadly, "Venu, I knew and honored your father, the rishi. I know he reared you in the best traditions. Revenge is not a worthy endeavor."

"How would I possibly locate him?"

"Venu, he is constantly accompanied by two bodyguards from the planet Maffia."

"I have never heard of the planet Maffia."

"It is as well. I am astonished that Allied Worlds allowed it to join. It is a planet of what amounts to assassins, soldiers of fortune, dealers in violence. It is as far from the traditions of Harappa as it is possible to get. It is a nothing world."

Venu rubbed his hands up and down his jodhpurs. "I realize that I am but a young man. Where could I find someone to assist me in finding this Hari Maroon and confronting him?"

Rana Kumbha sucked in breath. "Your father was a friend, as well as my superior. I cannot but accept his son. But vengeance, as Lord Krishna has told us, is a sad path."

"Where can I find a man of violence to assist me?"

"Nowhere on Medea."

"Where?"

Rana Kumbha sighed again. "There are professional condottiere, soldiers of fortune, private eyes, if you will, to use the old idiom, on various backward worlds. They are for hire, mercenaries. The sister planet of Medea—Tangier—has various of them. It is a refuge planet; there are no extradition laws. A criminal is safe on Tangier. As safe, that is, as anyone else on Tangier. It is a barbarian world."

"Do you know of any of these men?"

Rana Kumbha said unhappily, "Yes. Several. There is Billy Hichock, a professional assassin. There is West Hawkins, who is wanted on a dozen worlds and by Interplanpol."

"Interplanpol?"

"Interplanetary Police, of Allied Worlds, whose home planet is Earth. Tangier is the only world that does not allow them to operate. So long as one does not offend Tangier law, one is welcome to remain there, at least so long as one has resources. It is a strange planet. Most of its interplanetary credits are derived from refugees who have nowhere else to go. They are, if you will remember the idiom, on the run."

"I see. And of them all, who is the most . . . most efficient man of violence?"

Rana Rumbha thought. "It is not a subject with which I am well acquainted. However, I have heard of a man named Whip Gunther. If I am not mistaken, your father, the rishi, once utilized his services—before he became a fugitive."

"My father!"

The interplanetary trader shook his head. "Your father was not an opportunist, Venu Jhabvola; however, he served his home world. When he met with unscrupulous adversaries he was not above meeting fire with fire. I might say that I have never met a Harappan who did not honor your father. Nevertheless, he was a man of strong opinions who never shrank from doing what he thought was needed to defend the interests of our world."

"Where can I find this Whip Gunther?"

"He is on Tangier, but you might as well forget about him."

"Why?"

"He is wanted by practically everybody, including Interplanpol. The moment he left Tangier, he would be seized."

Venu lowered his head into his hands. "It makes no difference. I could not journey to this planet Tangier, even if I wished. Not to speak of hiring this man of violence. My uncle, the acting rishi, gave me no interplanetary credits whatsoever save my fare to and from Medea from Harappa."

The other was staring at him. "No interplanetary credits? But you are the son of Rishi Sudhin Jhabvola. His oldest son?"

"I am his only son."

"Then you are one of the richest men of Harappa."

"No. I would think you would be aware of the fact that my father's supposed wealth is actually that of the Expediter sub-caste, which is, of course considerable. But my uncle Mulk is now acting rishi and I am penniless."

The other was still viewing him strangely. "Son of my friend," he said, "your father evidently never informed you, but in his dealings among the many worlds, he made private investments. Sometimes, due to his inner knowledges in interplanetary affairs and as an expediter, they were unbelievably profitable. He once told me, in a saddened frame of mind, that the children of persons ranking as highly as he did could be faced with disaster. Hence it was that he deposited his private profits in the banks of the planet Geneva, the interplanetary banking clearinghouse. Young Venu, you are probably one of the wealthiest persons in Allied Worlds. You and your sister. I have forgotten her name."

7

Venu Jhabvola's trip from Medea to Tangier presented few difficulties. He'd had to remain on the world where his father had disappeared only for one night, which had involved his staying in a hotel for the first time in his life. Back on Harappa, if he ever took a journey which involved his sleeping away from home, he invariably had relatives or other members of the Vaishya caste who would gladly extend their utmost hospitality to him.

Rana Kumbha had taken over the details of seeing that his father's account, in Geneva, was transferred to his name. It was mere formality, in spite of the fact that he was underage. Evidently, Sudhin Jhabvola had taken measures to insure that his son could inherit, no matter what his years.

It was a strange feeling for Venu. He had never possessed more than a small allowance, since his father was desirous of teaching his children the value of exchange, and the vanity of ostentatious living. But now that the young Harappan had all but unlimited interplanetary credit, expendible upon any of the Allied Worlds, he could think of nothing he wished to buy, other than what services he might need to either find his father or revenge him.

For vengeance he was determined upon, in spite of what Rana Kumbha had said as to the unworthiness of the emotion. Even though he would lose merit, and upon his next reincarnation be degraded, he was determined upon it.

Rana Kumbha had found him a room in the Hotel Medea, a swank hostelry largely devoted to interplanetary travelers. So it was that Venu was able to witness the costume and sometimes strange languages of a score of worlds, in the lobby and other public rooms. Amer-English, indeed, was the most prevalent tongue spoken, but far from the only one. Venu was fascinated. Save for a few occasions when he had met, through his father, delegations to Harappa from other worlds, he had seldom indeed heard anyone speak in a language other than his own, which was itself Amer-English. When the colonists had left Earth to settle Harappa, they had mirrored Mother India in that they spoke fourteen major languages and over a hundred dialects. The only answer was to adopt a lingua franca, and Amer-English was chosen.

The first officer of the *Hammerfest IV* had been correct about the lack of appreciation of the arts on Medea. All of the arts, including cuisine. Venu had gone down to one of the hotel restaurants out of curiosity, but had not even gotten so far as to take a table. He was repelled by the food he saw before the diners. Practically every dish seemed to be dependent upon meat. Meat! Real meat! He had no illusions about what it was, not only through smell, but in actuality one could see the form of the bird, or small animal, on many plates. By the sacred fire, Agni, these people were cannibals! How could they know but that the chicken or other fowl or beast one ate might be the reincarnation of a dear relative?

He returned to his room and investigated the hamper the chief steward had given him. The other had been considerate enough, when Venu had first boarded the *Hammerfest*, to enquire about his eating prejudices, and had gone far out of his way to provide a vegetarian diet for the Harappan. And now, when Venu checked, he found the picnic basket full of fruits and vegetables and sweets, some of them cooked and in containers, but all of them cold by now, of course.

He made a satisfactory repast and decided that he might as well continue to carry the hamper. From time to time be could replenish it, undoubtedly, but if they dined on Tangier as they did on Medea, he doubted if he would ever get by in a restaurant. He could not trust any dish not to be possibly flavored with animal or fish or extracts from them such as fats or oils. No, he could not defile himself by exposure to such fare.

Following his meal, he was for a moment nonplused over what to do with himself until bedtime. He had no desire to go sight-seeing about the capital city of Medea. Thus far, he had seen nothing to interest him on the planet of the Technocrats. All seemed to be commercial and drab, fast-paced and industrial. He decided, instead, to descend to the public rooms again and see what he could find in the hotel bookshop in the way of a guide to Tangier. He feared that he was going to have his troubles locating this Whip Gunther. There was not even a Harappan embassy on the refuge planet where he might have found assistance.

They did, indeed, have a small guide to Tangier. He put the booklet on his hotel bill, to be paid for the following day when his interplanetary credit was established, and started back for his room.

The attack came as a complete surprise. He had, of course, not expected it, and hence, had not taken even the slightest of precautions.

He had been only half aware of the fact that another had ridden up in the elevator with him. All he could have said about his fellow passenger was that the man was dressed in standard Medean garb.

The blow struck him on the back of his head. The book fell from his hands onto the carpeting of the hotel corridor. Venu went down onto his knees and then, blacking out, on his face, sprawling.

8

A voice came from a great distance. There was the voice and someone shaking his shoulder.

"Boy . . . young man! How are you?"

He opened his eyes, dazed. "What . . . what . . ."

There was a man beside him, down on one knee, and a woman standing. The woman was staring down the corridor. "He went around the corner there," she said, her voice high.

The man said, "Are you all right?"

Venu sat up. "What . . . what happened?"

"Our room is further down. We came around the corner of the hall just as he was striking you on the back of the head. He had some sort of bludgeon in his hand."

"Bludgeon?" Venu muttered. He shook his head, still dazed.

The other took him by the arm and helped him to his feet. "Yes, we surprised him. He turned and ran."

Venu's rescuers were a very ordinary pair, fairly elderly. They must have been interplanetary tourists, or perhaps traders from another planet, since their dress was of a type Venu had never seen before.

He said, "I don't understand. This . . . assailant. What did he look like?"

The man had stood too, still holding the Harappan youth's arm to steady him. He was looking at Venu in a queer way.

"I don't know. It all happened so quickly. He hit you, and when you fell, began to bend over you as though he was about to hit you again. Do you have an enemy who would do such a thing?"

Venu shook his head. "I know only one person on this whole planet, a friend of my father's at our embassy. Perhaps this man wished to rob me."

"Rob you of what? On Medea they utilize a universal credit card. Or, if you are from another world, an interplanetary credit card. There is no money, and you obviously wear no jewelry. Do you carry anything of interest to a robber?"

Venu shook his head. "No. Not that I can think of." He bent and retrieved his book.

He bowed to them. "May Lord Krishna reward you for your kindness to a stranger. Undoubtedly you have gained merit on your way to Nirvana."

"Wait a minute," the man said. "Aren't you going to notify the police?"

Venu Jhabvola shook his head blankly. "What would I tell them? I didn't see this stranger, nor can you describe him. And he is gone. If I notify the police, perhaps they will detain me to find why it should be that I brought on a seemingly unprovoked attack. And I must be on my way tomorrow."

The woman was still flustered. She said, "But you should tell someone."

He bowed to her again, formally. "I will think about it in the quiet of my room, kind Shrimatee. May you reach moksha and Nirvana."

He turned away from them and stumbled toward his room, fingering the bump that was already rising on the back of his head.

What had his attacker wanted? Who could it possibly have been? True, he was embarking on a path of vengeance, but thus far he did not even know whom he pursued. Was it this Hari Maroon? He could suspect, but he did not know. All, thus far, was mystery.

Well, this was added mystery. If his attacker had not been interrupted, would he have killed Venu Jhabvola? In all his life,

Venu had not been exposed to physical violence. It was practically unknown on the Hindu world of his birth. Certainly, he had never thought in terms of being in danger for his life.

9

Rana Kumbha saw him off at the spaceport the next day. The interplanetary trade representative had gone out of his way to complete the arrangements for Venu Jhabvola's utilization of the credits in Geneva, to secure reservations for him on the space shuttle, and even hotel reservations in Meknes, the capital and largest city of Tangier.

Venu did not bother to tell him of the attack of the night before. What would be accomplished? There was nothing to report.

He said, "Good friend, do you have any idea of how I might contact this Whip Gunther?"

Rana Kumbha shook his head. "It is most likely that he is in Meknes, for Meknes offers the most on Tangier in the way of entertainment for one of another world. However, it is not necessarily where he would be. Indeed, if it were not for the fact that he would be in danger if he left the sanctuary of the planet of Tangier, I would say that I am not sure that he is there at all."

Venu nodded. "It does not seem the easiest thing to find one person on a whole planet."

But the takeoff of the shuttle spacer was being announced. He made hurried but highly felt thanks to Rana Kumbha and was on his way.

For the first time, on the shuttle spacecraft, he felt the full enormity of his position. It had not quite come through to him on the *Hammerfest IV*. Deep down within, he had secretly thought that he would find it all a great mistake. That when he landed upon Medea his father would be there to greet him and all would be as it had always been. And they would both return to Harappa to restore the life of the past, when Venu and Santha attended the university, and Sudhin was rishi of their family and sub-caste.

But now he could realize what a fool's dream that had been. And here was its immediate result. He was on a spacecraft headed for a sinister planet of which he had never heard before the first officer of the *Hammerfest IV* had mentioned it in passing.

So short a distance, in terms of space,

was Tangier from Medea, that they were in hyperspace only moments. They were setting down on the new planet almost before Venu had become adjusted to his velocity chair in the shuttle.

From the air, he could see why it was that this world had to depend upon fugitives to bring it the necessary credits to make purchases from other worlds. The planet seemed largely desert, with no bodies of water large enough to be called more than lakes, and precious little greenery of the type that blanketed Harappa. Venu wondered why human beings had ever settled such a miserable world. Could they not have journeyed on and found a more hospitable one?

At the spaceport, somewhat to his surprise, he found himself being paged. He had carried his suitcases and hamper to the administration buildings to check himself through the immigration and customs authorities. The porters, noting his youth and thinking him not good prey, had ignored him to take up the luggage of more prosperous-appearing travelers.

He held up a hesitant hand and was approached by a tall, evil-eyed type wearing a garment he was later to learn was called a djellabah. It was a hooded robe that descended all the way to the ankles and was made of a grayish, wool-like material. It

73

would obviously shed rain, be warm in the cool of night, but help repel the sun's rays during the day hours. Venu didn't know it, but the djellabah had originated in the desert lands of Earth long centuries before.

The other, at least, was a relief to Venu, in that his face was almost as dark as that of the average person on Harappa. Dark, but not otherwise the same; he had a huge curved nose and a long thin head.

He said, "You are, sir, Venu Jhabvola?" in passingly good Amer-English, though he pronounced Venu's name incorrectly.

"That is right," Venu said.

"I am from the El Minzah Hotel. Reservations have been made for you by Rana Kumbha of the Harappan Embassy on Medea."

Venu was pleased. At least he was not going to have to go to the trouble of feeling his own way through whatever local red tape prevailed.

"My name is Mohammed ibn Idriss, young sir," the other said, clapping his hands loudly.

Two youthful ragamuffins, clad only in dirty, baggy trousers and yellow, backless slippers, came hurrying up to take the two bags and the hamper.

"In my studies at the university in New Bombay I have read of the honorable prophet

74

for whom you are named," Venu said politely, following the other.

Customs and immigration officials were so lax on Tangier, Venu found, as to be all but meaningless. His guide saw him through in less than ten minutes. The officers seemed more bored than anything else. They all but yawned as they gave his possessions a cursory pawing.

Already Venu could see that the planet Tangier was just about as far from Medea as one could get. There was an ennui in the air, and there was obvious poverty. The two boys who were carrying his things couldn't have been more than twelve or thirteen and should have been in school. Instead, they were dirty and obviously, in their short lives, had missed many a meal. Venu was shocked. There was no poverty on Harappa and it had never occurred to him that there could be anywhere else.

Those he saw in the spaceport terminal that were not poor swung to the other extreme. Both men and women seemed to gleam with the oil of rich living, and they wore their position in both dress and ornament, far beyond the point which would have been considered seemly on Venu's own planet. In fact, in his eyes, they were in downright bad taste. Their garb was as colorful as that of Harappa, but garish, he thought, rather than having the gentle beauty of the flowing garments of home. Vaguely, he identified it as being related to the clothing of desert people of the far past on Mother Earth, the people of Arabia and North Africa, whom he had seen in historic Tri-Di television shows.

His guide, Mohammed, had a large hover-car waiting outside for them. He officiously saw that the luggage was put in the back, gave the two ragamuffins something that Venu did not see, and ostentatiously helped Venu into the right front seat. All of which Venu did not particularly appreciate, since on Harappa men did not ordinarily touch each other. It was not seemly, unless the other was a close friend.

On the way into the city of Meknes, Venu Jhabvola continued to be surprised. The countryside was largely barren. The few houses they passed—if they could be called houses—were tumbled down and drab. Such fields as were being cultivated were being done so by barefoot peasants working behind feeble-looking draught animals—donkeys, horses, even oxen. There were no such in New Bombay, save in zoos, or for riding as sport.

Mohammed, in his role as guide, kept up a running description of his planet, evidently not realizing that it did not compete favorably with other worlds.

"Many on the home world did not agree,"

he explained, "when the international zone was dissolved. Thus it was that our ancestors departed and . . ."

"International zone?" Venu said, trying to keep his inflection both courteous and interested, as behooved him as a younger person, even though the other was in a position of servitude to him.

"Yes, on Earth. The original city of Tangier, in the Shereefian Empire of Morocco. It was a paradise, so we are told by the scholars. For all practical purposes, there were no laws, no taxes, no restrictions on smuggling—which was an honorable profession, no extradition laws, so that each could come to the International Zone of Tangier and be secure from the authorities of other lands."

Venu looked at him. "No laws?" he said. "But suppose one person committed a transgression against another?"

Evidently, Mohammed's Amer-English was not as sufficient as all that. "Transgression?"

"Why . . . why suppose someone had attacked me upon the streets?" Venu had in mind the experience he'd had the night before on Medea.

Mohammed looked at him in surprise. "Why, the same as applies on this planet of Tangier, today. You would attack him back. You are, of course, armed? Surely a young sir of your years on your home world goes with adequate weapons."

Venu had never seen a death-dealing weapon, adequate or otherwise, in his life. He had seen them depicted in historic shows, usually with a sense of horror, but he had never seen a real one. Even the symbolic Sikh guards before public buildings on Harappa bore only pseudo-weapons. Their swords had no edge to them.

But he was on new ground and seeking vengeance. He said, biting his tongue to tell a falsehood, "Yes, of course."

They were now entering the city proper and Venu's eyes widened. The town was walled with medieval-type battlements. A huge horsehoe-shaped gate opened into the narrow streets beyond, and throngs of men, women, and children, often accompanied by burros or other animals, streamed into and from Meknes.

The highway they had taken from the spaceport narrowed as it approached the gate. But Mohammed, his guide, did not slow their pace for a moment. Their car dashed for the entry, the vehicle's horn going full blast. Venu winced and closed his eyes momentarily. However, Meknes pedestrians were obviously used to vehicles. They scattered out of the way at the last moment and the car sped through.

Mohammed ibn Idriss was proud of his

city. As they progressed along the narrow way, he pointed out the sights.

"That is the palace of the sultan, Moulay Ismail. He has spent a considerable fortune building walls, monumental gates, mosques, palaces. You must let me take you to the Kouba el-Khiyatine where he receives ambassadors from other worlds. That is the Er Rouha Mosque, where the sultan's family worships, and there the royal stables. And there is the bordj el-Heri Mansour, the barracks of the royal bodyguard. It has a gigantic octagonal hall surrounded by a sixteen-sided cupola. Over there are the monumental gates of Bab Mansour and Bab Djema En Nouar, which face on El Hedine square. And now we approach the Grand Zocco, the main souk."

Venu was wide-eyed through it all. "Souk?"

"Market, in Amer-English."

Venu Jhabvola had never seen such crowds of people, all scurrying about as though bent on desperate business. Had he known it, the city he was seeing had many of the attributes of the Baghdad of the days of Harun-al-Raschid. It would seem that every product produced anywhere on the 5,000 Allied Worlds must be on display for sale in shops that were often so tiny that the proprietor had to sit out front on a rug. Clothing of a thousand types, electronic equipment, jewelry, rugs and carpets, kitchen utensils, bicycles, weapons of a hundred varieties, some quite exotic, silverwear, tinware, food, drink . . . and on and on. Many of the traders had no stores at all, but had spread their meagre wares out on the sidewalks or streets.

At last the way widened somewhat and they pulled up before what Venu at first thought one of the numerous palaces they had been passing.

Mohammed, the guide, waved his right hand flowingly. "El Minzah Hotel," he said grandly.

A huge Negro, dressed in red with an orange turban on his head and an enormous scimitar in one hand, stood guard at the entry. Two boys came charging out, also in red, and seized Venu's baggage from the rear seat.

Venu preceded the El Minzah guide into the lavish lobby and to the reception desk, where a fawning clerk assigned him a small suite. The parade resumed and Venu was escorted to an elevator and up to the top floor of the establishment.

"It is cooler up here," Mohammed explained. "The breezes sometimes play."

Venu looked out the window, which oversaw an extensive garden, then about the room. The rooms were done in a Middle Eastern motif, he vaguely realized. Once again his knowledge came from historic

Tri-Di shows. He had always liked to watch those devoted to early Earth.

"It is very pleasant," he told Mohammed, then looked at the two bellhops. "But I have nothing with which to reward their efforts."

Mohammed put his two hands together and bowed unctuously. "It is always so with visitors from other worlds. The management simply adds a service charge to your bill. And if you wish local exchange, or any other kind of currency, there is a money dealer in the lobby. In exchange for your interplanetary credits, he can offer you any form of currency, credits, or whatever." He waved the two boys from the room, saying something to them in a tongue Venu did not recognize.

Venu said, "Any form of currency or credit? Why should I be interested in anything save the local legal tender?"

Mohammed beamed. "All currencies are legal tender on Tangier. You can buy and sell any currency or other medium of exchange—gold, silver, platinum, fissionable elements, whatever. You can also import or export anything, without a license. You can set up any business, without it being taxed. Tangier is a free port, such as has never been seen before. There are no smugglers, since there is no need to smuggle. There are few laws, and little crime, simply because so few things are criminal."

Venu was shaking his head in amazement. "But if there are no taxes, how can the government operate?"

"There is only an income tax levied on money made on Tangier." The other joined his hands together and bowed again. "And now, young sir, is there any service I can perform for you? I am yours to command."

Venu thought about it. He said politely, "You are most kind. I seek a man here on Tangier.'

"What is his name? Could you not simply call him on your pocket transceiver?"

"He is called Whip Gunther, but I am afraid that is a pseudonym. He is a man of violence who has sought refuge here on Tangier, due to your non-extradition laws. I do not know his Allied Worlds identity number, nor anything else about him."

The other's eyes narrowed infinitesimally. "Why do you seek him?"

Venu was instantly inwardly alert. The fewer persons who knew his business, the less likely it was that someone could warn his quarry. He said, "I cannot say."

The other nodded, evidently not surprised by the response. He said, "It is not to do him an ill? If I find him for you and he suffers as a result, then he might well take measures against me."

"It is not to do him an ill."

"Very well. I will seek him for you. I

believe I know of this man slightly. But it will be necessary to have some bakshish for the police."

"Bakshish?"

"A slight reward for the trouble they will be put to."

"Oh. Do the police on Tangier accept rewards for their services?"

"All authorities on Tangier accept rewards for their services."

"Very well. How much will be required?"

"Perhaps a thousand interplanetary credits."

"A thousand! Is that what you call a slight reward?"

"Such services do not come cheaply on Tangier, young sir."

Venu suspected that a considerable fraction of the slight reward would stick to the guide's own fingers, but there was nothing he could do.

He said, "Agreed. If you can find Whip Gunther, I will notify the hotel desk to transfer to your account, from my interplanetary account, that amount of credit."

"I fly to do your service," the other said in an oily voice, and was gone.

10

After the guide had departed, Venu spent his time in cleaning up, donning fresh clothing, and then supplying himself with a short repast from the food hamper. He noted that the supply was rapidly diminishing and realized that he was going to have to replenish it. Well, from what he had seen of the souk, as Mohammed ibn Idriss had called it, there was an abundance of fruit and vegetables available. The only thing was, he was getting terribly tired of this fare. He longed for a good curry and some curds, and his mouth watered at the idea of some dosa cakes of lentils.

In spite of the high bakshish that Mohammed ibn Idriss had demanded, his mission took him a very short time indeed. By the time Venu had finished his meal, the other had returned.

He flourished his hands dramatically. "It was as I informed you. Upon my promising a thousand interplanetary credits, the police were able to inform me of the whereabouts of this Whip Gunther."

Venu was relieved. "Good. Where can I find him?"

The other frowned. "Each evening, he is to be found in a caravansary in the medina, called the Bar Safari."

"What is a caravansary and what is the medina?"

"A tavern patronized by those from outerworlds. We followers of the Prophet do not take strong drink. The medina is the oldest part of town. Ah, the most disreputable."

"You mean that this man Whip Gunther indulges in al-kuhl?"

Mohammed eyed him. "From what I understand, this man Whip Gunther indulges in all the human frailties, young sir. I am told that he is possibly the most dangerous man on Tangier."

"I see. I have heard that he is a man of violence. But how can I find this Bar Safari?"

"I do not recommend it."

Venu looked at him, emptily.

Mohammed ibn Idriss said, "I could take you there . . . in return for a small amount of bakshish."

"What is a small amount of bakshish?"

The other hesitated, undoubtedly estimating how far he could go without raising the Harappan's ire. After all, it would presumably be possible to simply take a hovercab, even though the youth was a complete stranger to Meknes.

He said, "Perhaps fifty interplanetary credits."

Venu nodded, though he knew the amount exorbitant. "Agreed. You said he is present each evening. Would he be present now?"

The other looked out the window, to check the position of the sun of this system. "I would think so," he said.

"Very well, let us go."

"The young sir is armed?"

Venu pursed his lips. "Yes," he lied again.

They descended to the lobby and then emerged onto the street. Mohammed artfully flagged a passing hovercab and, with a flourish, opened the rear door for Venu. The driver, as evil-looking as Venu's guide and dressed almost identically save that he wore a woolen knit skullcap, looked back over his shoulder.

Mohammed spoke to him in the language he had utilized before the bellhops and they darted into the traffic. Night was coming on, but there seemed to be no diminishing of pedestrian traffic. It overflowed the sidewalks and largely took over the streets. The few vehicles there were invariably blaring away with their horns to clear passage.

Within a few minutes the streets narrowed and, if anything, the foot traffic increased. The buildings became shabbier. What windows there were were invariably barred with iron and sometimes had heavy wooden shutters as well. The resident of Meknes obviously did not trust his fellow man.

"The medina," Mohammed said, still the guide.

The street, now winding as though it had grown haphazardly rather than having been planned, was so narrow as to hardly afford them passage. Venu apprehensively wondered what would happen if they met another cab or other vehicle.

They emerged into a square packed with street vendors and a mass of humanity, their customers.

Mohammed said, "We shall get out here. It is the Petite Zocco. We can go no further by cab." He passed something up to the driver. Venu made no protest at the other paying. Thus far he had no local exchange, and besides, he had already come to the opinion that Mohammed ibn Idriss was not going to lose financially in his relationship with Venu Jhabvola, no matter what.

The hotel guide led the way to a passage so narrow that at first Venu thought of it as an alley, rather than a street. He could have reached out to each side and touched both walls simultaneously. It was unlighted save from what little illumination penetrated from the sky above, and that was rapidly becoming dark.

The street was empty of pedestrians. After about fifty feet, they came upon a decrepit sign which said, merely, *Bar Safari*.

"This is it," Mohammed said. "You should find Whip Gunther inside. This place has a very bad reputation. I will wait outside. If there is trouble I shall run for the police, who will possibly come to your aid when I tell them you are a very wealthy young man."

Venu looked at him. "Possibly?"

"Yes. This place has a very bad reputation," the other repeated.

Venu entered. The room beyond was not large. It held a bar with six stools before it, and three tables, each with four chairs. For some reason, hardly fitting in with the name of the establishment, the owner had attempted to give the bar a nautical air by draping a large fishing net from the ceiling and using an ancient ship's wheel for a chandelier. There were six persons present— the bartender, who wore a dirty white apron about his waist, three customers sitting at the bar, and two at one of the tables. All had drinks before them.

They looked up at his entrance, then, save

for the bartender, looked away again. None were dressed in the style of Tangier, and all were of lighter complexion than the usual man in the street. From other worlds, Venu decided. Undoubtedly some of the fugitives of whom Rana Kumbha had spoken.

The bartender said in a gravelly voice, "You're in the wrong place, Bud." He wiped the bar before him with a dirty rag.

Venu said politely, "I seek the Sahib Whip Gunther."

"What do you want with him?"

Venu looked about the barroom. From what little he had heard of the man he sought, none of these would fit the description. They were a furtive-looking collection. Surely none of them could be the most dangerous man on Tangier.

He said, "It is a matter of business."

The bartender grunted. "Whip could use some business." He gestured with his head at a door at the far end of the bar. "He's in there."

Venu bowed his thanks and headed for the door.

He hesitated at it, but in view of the fact that this was a public establishment, didn't knock. He turned the knob, pushed, and entered. Beyond was a small room, windowless, and containing nothing but a single table with several chairs about it. On the table was a half-empty bottle of some greenish looking potable, and next to it, a half-empty glass. A large man, bareheaded, was slumped over the table, his head in his arms. The room smelled abominably.

Venu Jhabvola was aghast. Surely this couldn't be the man he must depend upon to seek his father—or to revenge him. He stepped forward and put his hand on the other's shoulder to shake him into wakefulness.

The man suddenly exploded, coming to his feet, twisting quickly, his right hand a blur of motion. It darted into his clothing, Venu saw not where, and emerged with a vicious-looking weapon which was immediately trained upon the Harappan's belly.

Venu had once seen a historic Tri-Di show depicting the Viking discovery of America. Surely, this man could have performed in it. He looked more like a Viking than Eric the Red. He was perhaps two hundred pounds in weight, but far from obese. He was somewhat more than six feet in height, but moved as lithely as a panther. He was dark red of hair, which was cropped short, and blue of eyes, though these were now somewhat bloodshot. His nose had obviously been broken at least once, and there was a faint scar fanning from his hairline down to the left eyebrow. Perhaps he had once been handsome; now he looked as though life had given him a considerable buffeting.

The gun disappeared as neatly as it had materialized short moments ago.

The other took a deep breath and said, "Don't ever do that again, Sonny."

Venu Jhabvola pressed his hands together, the tips nearly touching his chin, and said, "Namastcy. You are the honorable Sahib Whip Gunther?"

The other looked at him blearily. "That's the first time I can remember being called that, Sonny."

"My name is Venu Jhabvola and I am of the planet Harappa."

Whip Gunther wiped his right hand over his mouth. "All right. Sit down. Have a drink. It's absinthe. One of the few worlds where you can get it."

Venu took one of the chairs and looked at the bottle unhappily. "We of my world do not drink al-kohl," he said.

Whip Gunther slopped some more of the evil-looking greenish beverage into the glass. "You must get awful thirsty," he growled. "What did you want with me? A young fellow like you, all dressed up like you were going to a party, isn't usually seen around a dump like the Safari."

"It is understood, sir, that you are a shikari of men."

Whip Gunther thought about that. "I've been called a lot of things," he slurred finally. "What's a shikari, or whatever you said?"

"It means hunter, sir," Venu said. "The profession of the shikari is an honorable one on the planet of my birth." He hesitated before adding, "Though we have no hunters of men."

The other shook his head for clarity. He had not survived in his way of life through the planets by being stupid.

"Do I understand that you've looked me up to hire a . . . a hunter of men?"

"Yes."

"Have you got any mazuma?"

"I beg your pardon, sir?"

"Don't beg my pardon, it makes me nervous. Mazuma, mazuma, the old dough-re-mi, bread, the old filthy lucre . . ."

Venu looked at him blankly.

"Money," Whip Gunther said bluntly.

"Oh," Venu said. "Why didn't you say so?"

"I did."

"Yes. I am amply supplied with interplanetary credits."

"How much is ample when you're hunting men? You don't look old enough to be slinging around any too much in the way of credits."

Venu said with dignity, "I understand I am one of the wealthiest persons on Harappa, which I understand is one of the wealthier planets in the Allied Worlds confederation.''

"Oh. You are, eh? Frankly, my own treasury is a little on the lean side. Who did you want knocked off, Sonny? Once again, you seem to be a little young to be making such deals.''

"Knocked off?''

"Killed,'' Whip Gunther said bluntly. "You said you wanted a shikari, a hunter of men.''

Venu was somewhat shocked. Although he had spoken of vengeance, he had not thought it out to the point of considering the violent end of whomever was responsible for his father's disappearance. Now he was forced to face what he was truly planning.

He said, hesitantly, "Perhaps I should have said, a seeker of men. At least for the present, Sahib Whip Gunther. I seek a man named Hari Maroon.''

"Hari Maroon! Then you'd better not find him. I assume you know who Hari Maroon is.''

"I believe him responsible for the disappearance of my father.''

"Then you'd better go on back to your Harappa, or whatever you called it, and go into suitable mourning for your dad. No man in his right mind goes up against Hari Maroon.''

Venu looked at him levelly. "You are afraid of this man?"

Whip Gunther finished his drink, sighed, and pointed to a gold ribbon, or band, around his right sleeve. "Don't you see that? Do you know what it means?"

Venu shook his head.

"It means that Interplanpol snagged me and gave me a dose of Nonvio. You know what Nonvio is?"

Venu shook his head.

"For somebody on the prowl for as hot a number as Hari Maroon, you don't know much about the strongarm business. Any person who has been injected with Nonvio can't harm any other living thing, not to speak of a man. You know what would happen if some bloodsucking insect landed on my arm right now?"

Venu shook his head blankly.

"I'd ask you to brush it off for me. I am physically and mentally incapable of harming any other life form. They used to throw characters with reputations like mine in jail. On some worlds they still do. In the far past, they used to execute them, and on some worlds they still do. But the Allied Worlds Interplanetary Police have come up with something far in advance of that. They simply treat us so that we are incapable of harming any other living thing."

He held up his arm and displayed the

golden ribbon. "We wear these in the way of protection. No decent man would pick a fight with anyone who has been given Nonvio. We can't even defend ourselves. Maybe we're looked at with contempt, but most people won't bother us—we're helpless."

Venu slumped in his chair.

Whip Gunther came to a decision. "Look, Sonny, you've obviously got a problem you aren't up to. I'll tell you what I'll do. Where are you staying?"

"At El Minzah."

Whip Gunther pursed his lips. "You *must* be loaded. All right. I can't take on finding Hari Maroon for you, but possibly I can give you some much-needed advice. You buy my dinner for me and possibly a few drinks and I'll answer any questions you want to ask and possibly toss in a few words of wisdom to boot."

"May the Lord Krishna aid you on your path to Nirvana," Venu said in thanks.

Whip Gunther stood. "I won't even ask you what that means," he said. "Let's go."

Venu followed him from the room and into the barroom. The other obviously had strong recuperative powers. There was no indication that only a few minutes earlier he had seemingly been under the influence of the green liqueur he had been drinking. In the barroom, the owner of the Safari said something to him which Venu didn't catch.

Whip Gunther growled, "I'll settle tomorrow," and held open the door to the street for his younger companion.

Venu passed through and into the now very dark alley beyond. He turned to the right, in the direction of the square Mohammed had called the Petite Zocco. There was no sign of his hotel guide. Venu assumed the other had made off, perhaps in fear.

Whip Gunther, coming up beside him, began to say, "Who brought you . . ."

But then the other suddenly launched out a heavy hand, sending Venu Jhabvola sprawling to the cobblestoned street. A pencil-lead-thin beam of light hissed out from a nearby doorway, missing the Harappan youth by scant inches as he fell.

Whip Gunther dropped to one knee. A beam, similar to the other, issued forth from his right hand in the direction of the doorway.

Bewildered, Venu staggered to his feet.

Whip Gunther, breathing deeply, walked with caution toward the darkened entry. There was a man sprawled there, a weapon a few inches from his outthrust arm. The big man stared down at him.

"Do you recognize this character?" he rasped to Venu.

The Harappan approached, still bewildered.

"Why . . . why it's Mohammed ibn Idriss, my guide from the hotel."

Gunther looked at him. "How long have you been on Tangier?"

"I arrived today. This man met me at the spaceport. He represented the hotel." Venu hesitated. "Or so he told me."

"If he did, then somebody got to him awfully quickly," Whip Gunther growled.

He looked up and down the narrow way. "Come on. Let's get out of here. The police are on the lenient side on Tangier, but they take a dim view of killing, especially when it's done by aliens. I wouldn't want to be invited to leave the planet."

He led the way toward the Petite Zocco, Venu scurrying along beside him to keep up.

"But what will happen to Mohammed?"

"Nothing will happen to him. Ever again. You don't survive a laser beam in the belly. Somebody will find him, probably not sooner than morning. One more body found in the medina. I doubt if anyone will care."

Venu was staring at him, partially in horror in reaction to what had just transpired.

"You said that you were incapable of even harming an insect. That the Interplanetary Police had inoculated you with what you called Nonvio. Is there any such thing as Nonvio?"

Whip Gunther pulled the gold ribbon from

his sleeve and stuck it into his pocket. He said, "Yes, there is, but I haven't had it. I wear this as protective coloring. It sometimes fools people. Maybe it fooled your friend back there. If he'd had good sense, he would have cut me down first, rather than aiming at you."

They had come to the street opening. Beyond, the Petite Zocco had begun to fall off considerably in the number of merchants and their customers. Many of the small stalls were being packed up for the night.

"Perhaps we can get a cab around here somewhere," Whip Gunther said. "Maybe not."

They did find a hovercab. In fact, it was the one that Venu and his supposed guide had arrived in earlier. He disliked the fact that the driver had seen him arrive in this area with Mohammed ibn Idriss earlier, and was now departing without him. If the other heard of the death tomorrow, he would undoubtedly be able to put two and two together, particularly if he knew the supposed hotel guide.

When they arrived at El Minzah, Whip Gunther got out first and looked up and down the street before allowing Venu to depart the hovercab. He paid the driver, who didn't seem to be more than normally interested in his fares.

They entered the hotel and wordlessly proceeded to Venu's suite.

Once there, Whip Gunther went through the living room, bedroom, and bath, before turning back to his younger companion.

"All right," he said. "Tell me more about it. What's this about Hari Maroon?"

Venu began to tell the story from the beginning.

"Just a minute," Whip Gunther said. "Harappa, Harappa. What did you say your name was?"

"Venu, son of Sudhin Jhabvola, rishi of the Expediters sub-caste of the Vaishyas."

The other looked at him narrowly. "You are, eh? I should have recognized your name sooner. Some years ago I worked for your father."

"So I have been told, though I know not in what capacity."

"A strongarm man," Gunther said gruffly. He looked about the room. "You haven't got anything to drink around here, have you? I'm beginning to die on the vine."

"I am sorry my hospitality is so inadequate," Venu said in dismay. "We of Harappa know little about beverages that contain al-kohl."

"Not even how to pronounce it," Wip Gunther said, wiping the back of his hand over his lips unhappily. He went over to the sideboard and took up the carafe of water that sat there and poured himself a drink. "It's pronounced alcohol."

Venu said politely, "It is according to how far back you go and what language you are utilizing. Al-kohl was first distilled in Mother India, and from thence was taken by the Muslims to the Near East and from thence the distilling process was infiltrated into Europe. It was the Arabs who dubbed in alcohol."

Whip Gunther laughed. "All right. I stand corrected. You're not as meek and mild as you look, and not as dumb. Let's get back to your father and what happened to him when he came up against Hari Maroon."

"What is a strongarm man?" Venu said first.

"A bodyguard, a pistolero, a heavy."

"I don't understand."

"Your father ran into some, uh, difficulties, on the planet Erginus. It was a trade deal he was expediting that involved several billion interplanetary credits. He did some sharp operating—all legal, but very sharp—that infuriated his competitors. They sent three bully boys to get him. He hired me to protect him until he was able to get off the planet, his work done."

"What happened to these three men of violence?"

Whip Gunther looked at him. "The last time I saw them, the very last time, they were in a swamp." He finished his water and added, "Face down."

Venu Jhabvola refrained from shuddering. Though this man had evidently protected his father, Sudhin, and possibly preserved his life, he could not find it in him to like the other. One did not take the lives of his fellow man. At least, one did not on the planet Harappa. What if all persons, throughout all of the Allied Worlds, were like this one? It would be a jungle. No person would be safe.

Whip Gunther took a chair. "All right," he said. "Let's get back to Hari Maroon and your father."

Venu seated himself on the couch and went into the story in full, bringing it up to the time he found Whip Gunther in the Safari.

When he was through, the other thought about it for a long, silent time.

Finally, he said, "Tell me about that attack on you in the hotel on Medea again."

Venu told him.

Gunther thought about it some more, once rubbing his right hand over his eyes wearily. He said, "Sonny, you've got more against you than you can handle. I don't pretend to know the answers, but you're up against some of the toughest men in Allied Worlds. And you're not just a young fellow, you're a young fellow without any background whatsoever in this dog-eat-dog mess you find yourself in."

"That is why I seek your assistance, Sahib Gunther."

The other sighed. "I can't help you." He shook his head. "Not for the reason I gave you before. The Nonvio story. That was, as I said, camouflage. The fact is, I can't leave Tangier. Interplanpol is waiting for me on most planets in the confederation. Where they aren't around, the local police authorities are usually looking for me, on, well more worlds than you know about. You can't get any more wanted than I am."

"But why is this so?"

"The night's not long enough to tell you about it. For everything in the book. For revolution on planets where they needed it, for serving in armed forces that lost, for killing people that needed killing, for armed robbery on worlds where a little armed robbery was necessary to feed people who needed feeding."

"I have read the Robin Hood legend," Venu said seriously.

Whip Gunther laughed. "You have, huh? Well, it's somewhat exaggerated. However, in my day I have shot a few people that at the time I thought could use shooting, but other people didn't think so, and I'm on the run. And this is the place you come to when you can no longer run. This is the end of the road. Tangier. If you can catch me off Tangier, I've had it. In spades."

Venu shook his head. "Not if you are a citizen of Harappa."

Whip Gunther looked at him and laughed again. "But I'm not a citizen of Harappa. I'm not a citizen of anywhere. I was born on Earth, but my citizenship was revoked when I participated in a war between Thesius and Hestione. It was quite a war, and I was a young fellow about your age, but the Earth authorities took a dim view of it. Citizens of Earth are not allowed to participate in wars, especially when they are between planets that are both members of Allied Worlds."

Venu said, astonished, "But there can be no wars between planets that belong to Allied Worlds."

"Theoretically," Whip Gunther said. "However, with five thousand planets belonging to the confederation, some of which are so far off that it takes a coon's age to travel back to Earth and the administration there, it can and does happen."

Venu said, "We return to the point. The point is that if we find my father has died of violence, then I am rishi of the sub-caste of the Expediters. If we find him alive, remote though that now seems, he is still rishi."

"All right. What's that got to do with it?"

"If I am rishi, I can adopt you into my

family and my caste. If my father is, he can adopt you. You would be not only a Harappan citizen, and safe from alien police, but a man of wealth."

Whip Gunther eyed him. "What if we don't find your father, either dead or alive?"

And Venu stared back at him. "Then you and I are both lost."

Whip Gunther came to his feet and paced the room. He growled. "You're a tougher kid than you first seem to be."

Venu held his peace. He did not feel like a tough kid, if he interpreted the other's words correctly. He neither felt like one nor wanted to be one. Right now, what he desperately wanted was to be back on Harappa, attending the University of New Bombay and living in the bungalow with his sister, Santha, and in the company of his friends Attia and Kamala.

The interplanetary adventurer was saying, "Hari Maroon is one of the most ruthless men going. He plays for keeps."

"But I have heard it said that you are the most dangerous man on Tangier."

Gunther snorted sourly. "Maroon is possibly the most dangerous man in Allied Worlds."

"You are afraid of him?"

Whip Gunther rubbed his mouth with the back of his right hand. "You're sure you don't have a drink around here?" And then,

"Of course I'm afraid of him. I'm not stupid. I'm a small-time operator. He could probably buy up a couple of worlds out of his petty cash and throw their whole military might around, wherever he wanted to throw it. He can stomp on somebody like me without bothering to remember he did it."

"When you spoke of him, I gained the impression you respected my father."

"Yes, damn it!"

Venu said nothing more, for the time.

Whip Gunther fished into his jacket pocket and came forth with a pistol. He handed it to Venu Jhabvola.

"All right," he said. "It's a deal. We try to find Hari Maroon, and through him, your father. If we pull it off, you adopt me. Offhand, I can't remember my parents, but I suppose you'll make as acceptable a one as either of them, although you're a bit younger, I imagine."

Venu looked blankly at the gun. "What is this?"

"That's the shooter that your friend Mohammed tried to do you in with. I picked it up, there in front of the Safari. Do you know how to use it, I should be so silly as to ask?"

"No."

"All right. I'll start instructions in the morning." He looked about the room. "I can sleep here, on the couch."

105

Venu tried to cope with the quick-moving events. "Perhaps that would be best. You must go to your own quarters and pick up your things."

Whip Gunther shook his head. "No. I'll have to ditch my things, as you call them. You see, Sonny, somebody is out to get you—but bad. And possibly they're already onto the fact that we've linked up. We'll never go back to the hole-in-the-wall I lived in and we'll get out of here tomorrow. If I had good sense, we'd get out tonight, but the El Minzah is the most expensive pad in Meknes and the best guarded. I think we're safe for one night."

11

Early in the morning, at first dawn, Whip Gunther took over, very efficiently.

He said, "Now, all these interplanetary credits you say you have. Can you get them out of Harappa to the extent we need them, or are they all tied up?"

"They aren't on Harappa, Sahib Whip Gunther. They're in banks on the planet Geneva and I have an interplanetary credit card."

"Just call me Whip, especially in view of the fact that if this all works out you're going to be my daddy. Fine. We're going to need credits. Lots of them. We'll have breakfast and then get out of here." He went over to the suite's order screen, saying over his shoulder, "How do ham and eggs sound to you?"

"I would prefer yogurt, fruit, and tea, Sahib Whip. On Harappa we do not eat the flesh of animals."

Whip Gunther looked at him. "It doesn't sound much like the kind of diet for a shikari of men. I'll stick to meat."

He gave the order into the screen, and shortly the center of the delivery table sank down to return with the food, napkins, and utensils.

As they ate, Whip Gunther said thoughtfully, "I know a place where we can hide out until we make arrangements."

Venu said, "What arrangements, Sahib Whip? How can we possibly find this Hari Maroon? He left Medea after finishing the business arrangements for the uranium and has disappeared."

Whip Gunther grunted. "Nobody disappears if he's still alive, Venu. Maybe he might try, and even stay undercover for a time, but if you want to find him badly enough and have enough credits to grease enough palms, sooner or later you can locate him. All right, let's finish this food off. Then get your things together."

Venu had little packing to do. He got his two bags and the hamper.

The other looked at the third piece of luggage. "What's that?"

"It is to carry my fruits, vegetables, and other foods that it is possible for me to eat."

The older man rolled his eyes upward. "You mean we've got to carry that all over with us, just because you can't eat ordinary tucker?"

Venu Jhabvola looked at him evenly. "On Harappa it is believed one gains merit in this incarnation by refraining from the devouring of our fellow life forms."

"All right. I wouldn't want to see you lose merit," Gunther said dryly. "Now this is what we do. Put your credit card on the order screen over there and tell them you want your bill immediately. They'll deduct the amount and we'll scoot out of here."

Venu did as he was told, somewhat shocked by the amount.

Whip Gunther brought out his laser pistol, checked it, and returned it to its place. Then he picked up one of the suitcases in his left hand and said, "You take the other bag and hamper. It's more important for me to have one hand free than for you. Let's hurry. For all we know, somebody is already taking steps to intercept us."

They hurried out into the hall and down it to the stairs, Whip Gunther's eyes darting in all directions. Considering his size, he moved with the grace of a cat.

Venu said, "Wouldn't it be faster if we took the elevator?"

"Faster, but not as safe. We're not going to the lobby, we're going to the basement."

The Harappan youth was slightly winded by the time they reached that destination, particularly in view of his load. But the big man didn't hesitate for a moment. He seemed instinctively to know where he was heading. They reached a circular steel steps and went up it to find themselves in an alley behind the hotel. They hurried along to its entrance.

Whip Gunther looked up and down the street before emerging. "This is the Rue Tarik," he said. "Not much traffic. But we'll walk a block or two before getting a cab. There doesn't seem to be anyone staked out back here. Possibly they haven't even found out yet that your pal Mohammed is no longer with us."

He kept up a rapid pace. At this hour, there were few pedestrians and even those showed them little interest. It would seem it wasn't polite on the planet Tangier to be inquisitive about the business of others. Venu was quite out of breath by the time they hailed a hovercab.

Whip Gunther said to the driver. "Kasbah."

Venu said, "Where do we go?"

"To the most disreputable part of town. The part of the medina up on top of the hill, where not even the police patrol after dark.

Every Arab town of any size has a kasbah. In the old days, it used to be the final fort where the local sultan or caid, or whatever, made his last stand if the city fell."

He was looking over his shoulder out the back window. "Nobody following," he muttered.

Venu was feeling an edge of excitement. It seemed a strange way to be trailing Hari Maroon. They seemed to be the ones who were being pursued, rather than pursuing.

They emerged from the medina wall through one of the enormous horseshoe-shaped gates, turned sharply right, and took the street paralleling the wall. The way began to rise quite steeply. After perhaps a mile, they came to another gate and swung through it.

"Kasbah," Whip Gunther said briefly. "From now on, we have to walk. Streets are too narrow for a hovercab."

Their vehicle had stopped. They got out and Whip Gunther paid the driver. They took up their luggage and started off again, this time down the winding, sinister alleys— Venu couldn't think of them as streets.

They wound about, up one narrow way, down another. They seemed to retrace their steps. Shortly Venu was so confused that he was convinced that he could never have found his way out of the area again.

Finally, they stopped before a large, dark

house, windowless on the ground floor. Whip Gunther looked up and down the street, which was empty, the day still being so young, and pounded on the door.

"Where are we?" Venu said.

"Home of Ahmed Abdallah," Whip Gunther told him. "He's a fixer. An operator. Something like your father—an expediter— but your father was honest."

"And Ahmed Abdallah is not? Then how can we trust him?"

Whip Gunther grunted. "He owes me a few favors, but that isn't what will motivate him. Your interplanetary credits will. Nobody on Tangier is honest, but all can be bought."

The door opened and a veiled woman dressed in what looked like a white bedsheet was there. She eyed them wordlessly, stood aside so they could enter. Whip Gunther cast his eyes up and down the alleyway once more and followed Venu inside.

He said, "Fatima, I desire to see Ahmed."

She turned and left, leaving them standing in the ornate entry. Once again, Venu was reminded of some of the historic Tri-Di shows he had seen of the old days of Morocco and Algeria, of Saudi Arabia and Iraq.

He was astonished at the interior of the building, as compared to the grim, forbidding exterior. One could never have suspected that a veritable palace lay behind those dirty walls. The roof was exquisitely decorated in blue, brown, red, and gold tile and the columns supporting it sprang out into arch form in a remarkably beautiful manner. The floor was covered with a rug so rich that Venu had never seen such, even on Harappa where the rug art was highly developed.

He said to Whip Gunther, who had put his bag down and was now obviously impatient, "How did you know her name was Fatima? Her dress was such that surely you could make out no features. It is ill that women should be made to dress so. It degrades them. There is an old Hindu proverb. Where women are venerated, the gods are complacent."

His companion said, "Well, they aren't venerated on Tangier. And with a Moslem woman, when in doubt, call her Fatima. Practically all of them are named Fatima, just like practically all of the men are named Mohammed. Fatima was the daughter of the Prophet."

The woman—at least Venu assumed it was the same one—came back and made a slight flourish with a hand to indicate for them to follow.

They followed her down a short hallway, through a small patio which featured an alabaster fountain in its center, to a comparatively small room beyond, which opened

113

onto the patio but had no windows. All light came through the door.

The room was quite spartan, as compared to the rest of the house that Venu had thus far seen, and was furnitureless, save for a few hassocks. A man dressed much as had been Mohammed ibn Idriss, but whose djellabah was of rich silk, was seated, cross-legged, on a red leather hassock. He wore a red fez.

At their entrance, he bowed his head slightly, touched forehead, lips, and heart with his right fingertips, and said, "My friend, the dauntless Whip Gunther. May your life be as long and flowing as the tail of the horse of the Prophet."

He was overly plump with a very fat mouth and very dark eyes, as dark as Venu's own. And, somehow, Venu felt, he was a man of evil and not acquiring merit in this incarnation.

Whip Gunther said, "Ahmed, this is a young friend of mine for whom I am working. Names will not be necessary."

The other took in Venu Jhabvola. "So be it. My house is your house. Welcome. Be seated effendis, and I will have Fatima bring mint tea." He clapped his hands, only gently, but the woman was there. He spoke to her in a language Venu did not understand.

Whip Gunther and Venu took the proffered hassocks and the interplanetary adventurer and the Meknes fixer, as Gunther had called him, exchanged meaningless pleasantries. The tea came on a great brass tray, and their host served.

The tea, Venu found, was so sweet as to be almost impossible, but the mint flavor was pleasant. It would seem they were going through a ceremony preceding business that Venu was not acquainted with, though his own people were also long on protocol.

When they had finished the third small cup of tea, Ahmed Abdallah put his cup down definitely. "And now, effendis, undoubtedly matters of great moment have brought you to my humble home. How can I serve you?"

Whip Gunther grunted amusement, and looked into the elaborate patio. "This is one of the least humble homes I think I have ever been in."

Venu was shocked at the grossness, but their host said smoothly, "Verily, you are too kind, Whip Gunther."

Whip Gunther got to business. "Ahmed, I'm going to have to leave Tangier."

The other bowed his head in acceptance. "Soon to return, I pray. There are, of course, ramifications."

Whip Gunther nodded to that. "I shall need a slight amount of plastic surgery. I need more than a slight amount, actually, but I haven't the time needed for healing of the scars."

The other nodded, as though it was the most reasonable suggestion that could be made.

"I also need false identification. An interplanetary credit card and the various other papers of some planet, any planet will do, so long as it is a member of Allied Worlds."

The other closed his eyes briefly in thought. "Do you have any interplanetary credits, my friend Whip Gunther? Because if you have not, your cover will be blown the first time you try to utilize the credit card. The computers are most difficult to confuse."

Whip Gunther looked at Venu, who nodded slightly to him. He said, "I'll have an amount transferred to my account."

"Very well. What else?"

"I want to find the whereabouts of Hari Maroon." Ahmed Abdallah's eyes were suddenly slits. "Why?"

"I am not free to say."

The Moor looked at Venu. "In this young man's behalf?"

"It is of no consequence."

"Friend Whip Gunther, verily, as all men know, one does not antagonize Hari Maroon."

Whip Gunther simply looked at him.

The Meknes wheeler-dealer sighed and said, "Do you have any idea where to begin? Hari Maroon is an elusive man."

"He was on Medea not too long ago. We don't know where he went. But he must have had to file a flight plan when he left. Do you have contacts in government on Medea?"

"Of course. But such information is classified."

"We are willing to pay for it."

The other's eyes were narrow again in his fat face. "What else?"

"We need a place to stay until all these things, including my plastic surgery, have been accomplished."

"I see. Are you being sought by the authorities, friend Whip Gunther?"

Whip Gunther laughed bitterly. "Friend Ahmed, as I thought you were aware, I have been sought by the authorities since I was a teenager."

"I mean, are you being sought by the authorities here in Meknes?"

Whip shrugged. "Perhaps, I killed a man last night."

"A citizen of Tangier, or an alien?"

"A citizen of Tangier."

"How sad. Verily, life is uncertain, as Omar said. Are you, ah, on the lam, as the antique expression has it?"

"Not so far as I know. The regrettable incident was not observed."

"Were you seen entering my establishment?"

117

"I don't think so."

Their host looked at Venu.

Venu said, "I do not believe we were observed."

Ahmed Abdallah said, "Perhaps you can stay here. However . . ."

"Yes, however," Whip Gunther said. "You owe me your life, on at least one occasion, Ahmed, but I am not asking for favors. Roughly, what will all these services amount to?"

The oily operator made a gesture of deprecation with a fat hand. "But for you . . ."

Whip Gunther rose cynically to the occasion. "No, my good friend, I insist."

The other thought about it, his plump lips moving in and out. "Including the necessary bakshish for the authorities on Medea, to learn the flight plan of Hari Maroon, one hundred thousand interplanetary credits."

"One hundred thousand! Are you mad?"

The other was firm. "You must realize that I run the risk of antagonizing Hari Maroon, if it is discovered that I have assisted you against his interests."

Whip Gunther looked at Venu, who was appalled. "Can you stand that?"

Venu steeled himself. "Yes."

Whip Gunther turned back to their host. "All right. Let's get to it. You know of a discreet physician who can perform the plastic surgery?"

"Of course, my friend."

Whip Gunther stood. "We will also need complete outfits. Clothes as inconspicuous as possible. Earth-style would probably be best."

Venu looked down at his familiar and comfortable achkan tunic and his jodhpurs. "But I have all the clothing I shall need, Sahib Whip."

Whip Gunther shook his head. "We don't want anything that indicates you come from Harappa. Our friends might be on the lookout for anyone from Harappa."

"It will be no problem," Ahmed Abdallah said, his voice oily as it always seemed when he was discussing money. "A few thousand more credits and I will outfit you in the style of two travelers journeying between the stars for pleasure or business."

"A few thousand credits!" Whip Gunther said. "What are you planning on clothing us in, diamonds?"

The other looked at him calmly. "You do not wish to be conspicuous. Anyone who can afford interplanetary travel is obviously wealthy."

12

The house was huge and seemed to consist of various patios, many of them with gardens or fountains, with windowless rooms opening off them in the same fashion as had the one in which they had met their host. Whip Gunther and Venu were assigned a small one in a remote wing, away from the bustle of servant activities. It had three rooms and a bath; two small bedrooms and one larger chamber for living and dining. The quarters were richly, though sparsely, furnished. There were no chairs. The beds were on low platforms, the bed clothes exotic. In the dining room, the table stood no higher than six inches, and there were hassocks around it for sitting.

They put down Venu's things and Whip looked about, his hands on his hips.

He said, "All right. You stay here while I prowl around a bit. I want to get the lay of the land on the off chance that we might have to get out of here in a hurry."

"Then don't you trust Ahmed Abdallah? We are in his hands."

"I don't trust anybody when my neck is involved," Whip Gunther growled, turning and leaving.

Venu sat down on one of the hassocks and brought the gun his companion had given him from his pocket. It was small but, to him, very vicious looking. He remembered how a beam of light had lanced out from it there before the Safari Bar, and how very crumbled Mohammed ibn Idriss had looked when Whip Gunther had cut him down with a similar ray.

He examined the death device carefully. He had seen guns, once again in historical Tri-Di shows, though Harappans were largely inclined to avoid this type of entertainment. He thus knew vaguely what the different parts of the weapon were—the barrel, the stocks, the trigger. He carefully kept his finger from the trigger.

"Look out," a voice growled. "You'll slice your foot off."

Venu looked up, startled. "I was merely . . ."

Whip Gunther took the laser pistol from

him and clicked the power pack magazine from its butt. He said, "I'll give you a rundown on using this later."

"I . . . I am not sure I wish to know," Venu said, a touch of defiance in his voice.

Whip Gunther sat down on a hassock across from the younger man. "Now look here, Venu," he said. "You're on the trail of Hari Maroon, who possibly did in your father. We'll probably catch up to him. When we do, there's going to be trouble. Now if you're unwilling to get into the scrap, if and when it comes, you'd better decide now and we'll forget about the whole project. So it's a matter of put up or shut up."

Venu's avoided Gunther's eyes.

"Well?" Whip Gunther growled.

"I accept your words, Sahib Whip. Please show me how one utilizes this device of violence."

"Okay. Now listen to this. It's a laser pistol, probably the most dangerous hand weapon ever devised. Unlike a gun that throws a projectile, such as a bullet, you don't have to make a bullseye. It throws a beam of light, as you saw last night, as you sweep it across your target, almost as though you were cutting. That gives you the advantage of not having to be a crack shot to bring your man down. You can, kind of, spray the whole vicinity. I'll have you operating this thing like a veteran before we leave here."

Venu closed his eyes in pain. "May the Lord Krishna forgive me," he murmured.

In the morning, Whip Gunther entered Venu's bedroom to find the boy kneeling beside the bed, his hands clasped together.

Venu was saying, "Lead me from the unreal to the real, lead me from darkness to light, lead me from death to immortality."

Whip Gunther looked at him and twisted his mouth. "What's all that?" he said as Venu came to his feet, his face composed.

"It is the Brihadaranyaka Upanishad 8, VII. 19."

"That tells me a lot."

Venu explained gravely. "The Upanishads are holy books which were composed in Mother India about 1000 B.C. There are about one hundred of them and they contain all the elements of Hindu thought. However, they do not constitute a compact philosophical system and are mainly poetic utterances on the nature of the Universe, social and ethical discussions, and metaphysical enquiries. These probings reveal the limitations of the human self and evolve the idea of the God-self which can be invoked to give absolute knowledge through direct inner experience."

Whip Gunther laughed and shook his head. "I can see we come from different schools.

When I was your age, I was learning such quotations as 'Never give a sucker an even break,' 'If I didn't do it, somebody else would,' 'Do your neighbor before he does you,' and 'There's a sucker born every minute and most of them live.' "

Venu said in horror, "By Agni, the sacred fire, surely you jest."

Whip Gunther sobered and, cocking his head slightly, said, "Are you sure? Besides, I said I was learning such quotations, not necessarily abiding by them."

He switched subjects and said, "The doctor's coming to chop up my face. While he's doing it, you might practice up on your laser. The one big thing you've got to remember is that range stud. One of these pistols will range up to about a half mile—if you let it. If your target is twenty feet away, don't let your beam reach out to fifty. You'll wind up cutting down a city block, and people can take a dim view of that. Always thumb your range stud to approximately the distance of the target."

"I will attempt to remember, Sahib Whip."

13

The next day, Whip Gunther's face partially bandaged, they were summoned to the informal office of Ahmed Abdallah. He was seated, as before, on his hassock, and again went through the amenities, including the three cups of tea, before getting down to business.

He said, finally, "I have heard from Medea, on the tight beam."

Whip Gunther looked at him. "Where did Hari Maroon go when he left that planet?"

Ahmed shook a plump hand negatively. "Verily, you are my good friend, Whip Gunther. However, as each man knows, business is business. There is the small matter of one hundred thousand interplanetary credits, plus five thousand for other services."

Whip Gunther scowled at him, but then turned to his young companion questioningly.

Venu said, "You have an account with the Geneva banks?"

"Yes, of course."

"You have facilities for transferring from my account to yours?"

From behind him, the Moor brought a small credit transfer screen with a hyperspace antenna.

Venu put his interplanetary credit card on the screen and his thumbprint on the identification square. He said, "The planet Geneva. I wish to transfer 105,000 interplanetary credits to the account of Ahmed Abdallah of Meknes, of the planet Tangier."

In approximately five minutes, during which time they remained quiet, the screen said, "Carried out."

Whip Gunther looked at their host. "All right. Where did Hari Maroon go when he left Medea?"

The other said levelly, "He came here to Tangier."

The interplanetary adventurer stared at him. "You mean he is on Tangier?"

Venu could hardly refrain from jumping to his feet.

But the Moor shook his head. "No. He left this morning."

"You mean he's been here and you didn't

let us know!" Whip Gunther was obviously incensed.

"That was not in our bargain, my good friend," Abdallah said. "Besides, if I had so informed you, you might have taken measures against him on Tangier, and a man of Hari Maroon's resources could easily have traced out the fact that I had acted against his interests. I am not a fool, friend Whip Gunther."

"Why did he come to Tangier?"

"I would not know. I would imagine to take advantage of our free-port facilities, to utilize some of our banking facilities, no records of which are kept on other worlds, not even Earth."

"Where did he go?"

The other looked at him, his fat face bland. "But that was not in our bargain either, friend Whip Gunther. I was commissioned to find where he went from Medea. Very well, I fulfilled my commission."

"Why, you Moslem pig!"

The other's eyes narrowed and he said, his voice oily, "I see you have studied our customs sufficiently, Whip Gunther, to know the greatest insult you can give me. So I will double the price I originally expected to charge you."

"Price for what!"

"For Hari Maroon's new destination. You see, I also have connections with the Meknes spaceport authorities. It will cost you one hundred thousand additional credits."

A silence fell. Finally, Venu brought forth his interplanetary credit card again and put it on the credit transfer screen. When the transaction had been completed, he looked back at the Moor.

Ahmed Abdallah said, "Hari Maroon is traveling in his private space yacht. He cleared from here to Elysium."

"Elysium?" Venu said. "I don't believe I have ever heard of this world."

"I have," Whip Gunther said. "In fact, I've been there. It's the only place I've ever seen Hari Maroon. And, now that I recall, I remember hearing that he almost always heads there after swinging a particularly profitable coup. I should have guessed that was where he would go." He looked at Venu in self-deprecation. "I would have saved you a lot of exchange."

"Such are the fortunes of finance," Abdallah said smoothly.

Whip Gunther's eyes came back to him. "All right. But the rest of our bargain. Where are my forged papers, my interplanetary credit card, and my identity documents?"

The other fished into his djellabah and brought forth the papers in question. "I must remind you again that, unless you actually have interplanetary credits to your account, the first time you use this the computers will check it out and the authorities will be after you."

Venu said evenly, "He will have credits to his account."

Whip Gunther said, "When does the next spacer leave Tangier for Elysium?"

"In two days," Ahmed Abdallah said. "But, of course, you will not be able to take that. Your face will not have healed. The next leaves in approximately a month. For a small sum you can remain here until . . ."

"We'll have to take the first one," Whip Gunther said grimly. "Otherwise, by the time we reached Elysium, Hari Maroon might have gone on to some new destination and I'm not sure we could find someone there that would sell out his flight plan."

The interplanetary adventurer came to his feet. "Will you make reservations for us?"

"But your face."

"There are no representatives of Inter-planpol on Tangier. There'll be nobody at the spaceport who'll be curious when we leave. And by the time we reach Elysium, I can hope to be able to remove the bandages. It's not the kind of world where the local authorities are overly curious about their visitors. They can't afford to be. Our only obstacles will be if any Interplanpol men are at the Elysium spaceport giving more than a cursory examination to identity papers. How much of an inspection will these forged papers stand?"

"Not much," Ahmed Abdallah admitted. "All they have to do is check back to your supposed home planet to discover that you don't really exist." He added grudgingly, "Your interplanetary credit card is better. The planet Geneva doesn't care if you exist or not, just so long as your account has credits."

"Make the reservations," Whip Gunther sighed.

14

Back in their quarters, while they prepared for their midday meal, Venu said, "Why should it be that the local authorities on Elysium are not overly curious about their visitors?"

"They wouldn't want to scare them off. Elysium is a pleasure world. There are several of them in Allied Worlds, but Elysium is probably the farthest out."

"Pleasure world?"

"That's right. One big resort. Practically the whole economy is based on supplying pleasure to visitors from other planets. Obviously, anybody who can travel between the stars, other than spacemen, is wealthy. Many of them can't throw the type of winging on their home planets that they like, particularly if they come from one of the religiously dominated or otherwise conservative worlds. So they come to Elysium and spend small, and sometimes not so small, fortunes on having a good time."

"But what sort of pleasures would induce anyone to travel so far to indulge in them?"

Whip Gunther looked at him and laughed. "You're too young to understand, Venu. But that's sometimes the thing about the very rich. They start experiencing their jollies in all-out fashion early in life. When they've reached their middle years they've done just about everything there is to do in the way of having fun. So they begin looking for new thrills, more exotic pleasures, really far-out stuff. Well, Elysium tries to provide them."

Venu Jhabvola was frowning. "I am not so young as all that, Sahib Whip. And if I am going to this world, surely I should know something about it. What do you mean by far-out stuff?"

Two of the servants were beginning to bring in dishes and to put them on the low table. Whip Gunther and Venu sat cross-legged, which was the only possible way to eat from such a table. Before Whip Gunther was an enormous cous-cous, the somewhat rice-like cereal which originated in the Near East of Earth long centuries before. It was covered over with chicken and sauce, and over that was sprinkled sugar and cinnamon. The first time he had eaten it, Whip Gunther had been set back by the sugar over a meat dish, but he was now as fond of cous-cous as any other food he had ever eaten on Tangier.

Before Venu were several dishes of fruits and vegetables, some cooked, some fresh. How he would have liked a well-done, highly spiced curry! He sighed and reached for an orange.

His companion thought about his last question. "Well, they have gambling. They have every kind of gambling I've ever heard of, and the highest stakes. I've seen an ultra-rich tycoon from the planet Catalonia drop a million interplanetary credits on one horse race, and never blink an eye. Then there are the most exotic foods from every world in Allied Worlds. And there's every drink I've ever heard of, and I've heard of a lot of them."

Venu was frowning. "Thus far, you have said a great deal about extremely expensive pleasures, but nothing that would seem to live up to your expression 'far-out stuff.'"

"All right, here's one for you," Whip Gunther said around a large chunk of chicken. "You can obtain just about any narcotic used anywhere in Allied Worlds."

Venu was shocked. "But that is against interplanetary law! It is against the Allied

Worlds Covenant pertaining to giving interplanetary travelers addictive drugs."

The big man laughed. "Thus far, Elysium has gotten around that by a cute trick. You can take any narcotic known to man on Elysium, but before you leave you first have to take the cure for addiction, and then they brainwash you to the point of having the memory of what drug you were taking wiped out. So, they point out, nobody gets addicted on Elysium and hence the drugs they take aren't addictive."

"And you say that this Hari Maroon goes to Elysium after each of his financial . . . adventures? He must be a very corrupt man."

Whip Gunther chuckled. "I've been there a few times myself, when I could afford it, which, admittedly, isn't very often. There are other attractions on Elysium besides taking narcotics, and picking up some of the most beautiful girls on 5,000 worlds. For instance, they can afford to import the best entertainers anywhere."

It was at that moment that the two assassins darted into the dining room, knives drawn.

Venu sat there, frozen, his eyes staring. He would have been simple prey.

But the two bearded Moors must have realized that and for the moment ignored him, dashing toward Whip Gunther, their long, curved knives on high.

However, they were dealing with he who had been called the most dangerous man on Tangier. Big though he was, Whip Gunther seemed to bounce off the hassock on which he sat. Up to his feet and then back, until he was against the wall.

Once again, Venu Jhabvola witnessed the interplanetary adventurer move so fast that his hand seemed a blur as it plunged into a side pocket.

What transpired then came so fast that Venu could never remember the picture clearly. One of the two Moors, attacking, was impeded by the hassock upon which Whip Gunther had been seated. Cursing, he stumbled around it, heading for the big man.

The other was almost upon his victim, who stood up against the wall. Then Whip Gunther extended his arm and what looked like a snake extended out from his hand. Its head slashed into the attacker's eyes. The man screamed, dropped his knife, and fell to his knees.

The other had circumvented the hassock and was upon his supposed victim.

But Whip Gunther had snapped his weapon back so that now he held one end of it in each hand. He banged it down upon the other's knife wrist. He quickly twisted his hands so that his device was around the other's wrist and forced the man to the floor. He let loose one end of the strange object, freeing it from the wrist, brought it up high, and then down on the fallen man's temple.

He strode quickly across the floor and slashed down at the man he had blinded earlier, hitting him over the head and collapsing him completely.

He snapped to Venu, "All right, let's get out of here before we run into more trouble! Get your things!"

The order brought Venu Jhabvola out of his daze. He came to his feet.

"But . . . but what has happened? Who are . . . ?"

Whip Gunther, already heading for the door, snarled, "No time. Let's go!" The thing he had beaten the two assassins with flicked back into his palm and he dropped it into his pocket. Venu could see it was some sort of chain, about two feet long, with weights on either end.

The Harappan hurried back to his bedroom and as quickly as possible stuffed the new clothing Ahmed Abdallah had provided into his bags. He took them up, along with his food hamper, which he'd had replenished by the kitchen servants. He was overburdened, in their clumsiness, but scurried back into the patio.

Whip Gunther was already there with his

own two bags. To keep his right hand free, he had both of them under the other arm.

"Come on," he snapped. "Out of here. This way. Thank God I scouted the route when we first arrived."

Venu followed him on the trot.

He said, breathlessly, "Shouldn't we inform Abdallah?"

His companion laughed bitterly, and didn't bother to answer. "Down this corridor!" he ordered needlessly, since he was leading the way. "Up here," he said, going up some stone steps.

They emerged on a roof with a parapet. Whip Gunther stared down over the side.

"Empty," he said. "Leave your bags. You go first, on the off chance somebody is following us."

Venu stared down at the alley below them. It seemed a long drop. He sucked in his breath.

Whip Gunther snarled, "Over the side and hang by your hands. Flex your knees when you drop. When you hit, roll out."

Venu followed orders as best he could. For the briefest of moments, he hesitated before letting his hands go. He hadn't known what the other had meant when he said roll out, but he did when he hit. He began to fall over forward, but relaxed his body and rolled.

Whip Gunther called from above, "All

right. Here come the bags. Try to catch the hamper, or it'll break open. In fact, try to grab them all as they come down. There are a few breakable things inside."

He dropped them one by one, then vaulted over the side of the parapet, landing lithely on his feet. He grabbed up his things under his left arm and snapped, "All right, let's go. Let's get out of here."

He seemed to know the way. Venu followed him clumsily down the alley, into another alley, up it. It was a repetition of the other day when they had come to the Kasbah for refuge. Now they were evidently escaping it.

"Where are we going?" Venu puffed.

Whip Gunther grunted. "Back to the El Minzah Hotel, along with our new identities. We're going to have to hole up there until that spaceship leaves for Elysium."

15

Back at the Minzah, they had no difficulty in registering. In fact, the two-bedroom
suite they were given was on the same floor
as where Venu had first stayed.

The reception clerk had looked only mild
askance at Whip Gunther's bandaged face.
"Accident," that worthy had said briefly.

There had been little time for conversation since they had escaped over the wall of
the house in the kasbah but now Venu said,
"Why did we return here? Whoever are enemies are, surely they will be able to find us
again in this place."

Whip Gunther sat down at the living room
desk. "It's as good a pad as any. The boys
after us would be able to locate us wher-

ever we went and at least El Minzah is well guarded."

He flicked on the order screen and put a call through to the spaceport. In a few minutes he looked up at his younger companion. He said, "I'll be darned. Abdallah put through those reservations for us on the spacecraft to Elysium."

"He said that he would."

"Yes, but what would the point have been if those two killers had succeeded in their job?"

"You think him responsible for them?" It hadn't occurred to Venu.

Whip Gunther rubbed the back of his hand over his lips. "It doesn't seem very likely that they could have gotten into his house without him knowing it, and, even if they had, how would they have known where to locate us without his being in cahoots with them?"

"But he fulfilled his bargain."

The other nodded. "Yes. Ahmed has his code of ethics, in his own strange way. He has to have. This is a queer world, Tangier, but if the word went around that wheeler-dealer Ahmed Abdallah reneged on a bargain he had made, he'd get precious little in the way of deals in the future. But that doesn't prevent him from looking up Hari Maroon and making another deal with him. A deal to have us both bumped off. Or possibly just a deal to let two of Maroon's boys into the house where they could do us in."

"I was surprised, Sahib Whip, that you did not use your laser pistol upon the two assassins."

Whip Gunther grunted. "I couldn't afford to. It's practically impossible to only wound a man with a laser beam. You're almost sure to kill him."

"But they were attempting to murder us."

"Ummm. But the Tangier police still take a dim view of aliens killing local citizens. It might have taken us a time to clear ourselves, and that spaceship leaves in two days. We have no time for loal hassles. No, all I could do was bang them up a bit."

Venu looked at him curiously. "That was a very strange device you used, Sahib Whip. I have never seen such a thing before."

Whip Gunther dipped into his side pocket and brought it forth. "Few pople have," he said, "which is one of its advantages. It comes as a surprise. It's a manrikigusari. It was invented a long time ago in a country named Japan, on Earth."

He handed the thing over to his companion, who examined it carefully, though with a touch of distaste on his face. It was made of a Number 3, straight welded link machine chain, on each end of which was a hexagonal weight attached with a swivel.

The big man was saying, "It takes a lot of

practice, but once you're onto the manriki-gusari it becomes one of the most vicious hand-to-hand combat weapons that has ever been invented. You can take a man with a knife, a sword, or a club in split seconds. That first attack you saw me make is called the kasumi. Very basic. With the manriki-gusari concealed in the right hand, you step forward with the right foot and throw it straight forward, extending the right arm in a snapping movement to the front, as though you were thrusting with a short knife. You, of course, hold on to one of the weights, so you can bring it back again. The object is to strike the guy in the eyes and face with the other weight. It puts them out of action quickly."

Venu shuddered and handed the thing back. "Why did you ever learn to use such a terrible thing, Sahib Whip?"

Whip Gunther returned the chain to his pocket and said, wryly, "So others wouldn't use some equally terrible things on me. You can kill with it by hitting various vital spots, such as the temple, or use it to strangle with, but largely it's a defensive weapon."

Venu turned and went to the window and looked down into the garden, thinking it out. Earlier, he'd had a faint suspicion that Whip Gunther and Abdallah had been working together to extract large sums of interplanetary credits from a young Harappan youth who was not up to their Tangier standards. But now it was obvious that his doubts had been unfounded. The big adventurer, this shikari of men, had proven himself worthy of his hire. Twice now he had defended Venu's life at risk of his own.

Venu turned to him and said, "Sahib Whip, do you think there will be other attempts upon us before this is through?"

"Yes." The word came out bluntly.

"Is this why you hesitated to take the assignment when I first offered it to you?"

"Yes."

"Do you think we will succeed?"

"No. It's like I told you, Sonny. Hari Maroon is the most dangerous man in the federation. How he learned about you and what you're up to, I haven't the vaguest idea. But he did, and now he's out to stop you."

"Then I release you from your pledge to assist me, Sahib Whip. If I had known how difficult was the road I follow, I would not have exposed you to the dangers. It is more than a man should be asked."

"Oh? You do, eh? And how about yourself?"

"I shall continue, to either find my father, or take vengeance on whoever destroyed him."

"I see. Well, a deal's a deal, Venu, and you promised to adopt me into Harappan

143

citizenship and to make a wealthy man out
of me to boot. And I'm going to hold you to
it. It's the best offer I've had for years."

"But . . ."

"No buts about it."

16

Somewhat to Whip Gunther's surprise, no further attempts were made upon them while they remained on Tangier. He took every precaution, but so far as he could see they were unnecessary. They remained in their rooms for the whole two days, ordering their meals from the highly automated kitchens below and having them delivered through the automatic table. They allowed the maids to enter to clean up, but only after carefully checking them.

They left the hotel two hours before the spaceship *John Shepherd* was scheduled to blast off. It couldn't have been easier. The hotel's hover limousine took them and Whip Gunther had the driver approach to within a few feet of the vessel's gangplank.

They hurried up it, Whip Gunther wanting to get into the safety of the interior as quickly as possible. There could always be a long-range sniper waiting for them to expose themselves.

At the top of the steel gangplank was one of the ship's officers, clipboard in hand. He looked at Whip Gunther's bandaged face somewhat in surprise.

"Accident," Whip Gunther said. "I'm Warren Beattle and this is Venu Jhabvola. We have reservations for Elysium."

"Of course. Your compartments are 25 and 26, which are adjoining. You will eat at the Chief Engineer's table." He snapped fingers and two stewards materialized. He said to them, "Mr. Beattle and Mr. Jhabvola, Compartments 25 and 26."

The stewards took up the luggage and led the way down metallic corridors. Whip Gunther gave a sigh of relief once they were inside.

The SS *John Shepherd* was considerably more elegant and comfortable than had been the *Hammerfest IV*, but it was just as boring a trip, Venu found. Although there were possibly a hundred passengers with whom to talk and play games, he rather missed the informal company of First Officer Tryggvason and the others on the space freighter.

Largely, he associated with Whip Gunther

and the interplanetary adventurer regaled him with tales of other worlds. Somehow, most of the stories had a humorous twist. He seldom mentioned his more dubious actions. Possibly, Venu thought, it was because he knew that Harappans abhor violence. He didn't know that few real men of action like to talk about combat and death. It is sufficient to have to live through it.

Whip Gunther insisted that they continue to practice with the laser pistol. The power cell removed, he trained Venu in the quick draw. He taught him how to use a sweeping beam when more than one opponent was involved. Above all, he drilled home the fact that before the trigger could be pulled it was necessary to flick the range stud to approximately the correct distance of the target. Otherwise, all else beyond could become a shambles. The laser pistol was no toy.

He at first also tried to teach him the elements of the deadly fighting chain he carried in his pocket, but soon gave up. Since they only had one chain between them, and it was unlikely that Whip Gunther would ever give his up, it wasn't of too much importance.

He gave the Harappan a brief course in karate, but Venu simply couldn't bring himself to deal a blow of sufficient force to make any difference. The professional soldier of fortune was disgusted.

"What would happen on your world," he demanded, "if somebody socked another on the nose?"

"Socked?"

"Hit him."

"Why . . . why the one who was hit would be amazed, and concerned for the other."

"Concerned for the other! How about his concern for his bloody nose?"

"Why, surely that would be of minor importance, in view of the fact that his assailant must be mentally deranged."

Whip Gunther rolled his eyes upward. "And we're out after Hari Maroon," he groaned.

Of all the passengers, only eight others were embarked for Elysium. Venu's first instincts were to avoid them because of their obvious hedonistic tendencies, their sensuousness. To him they were objectionably gross in their appetites. They were going to Elysium for the reason practically all other-worlders went to Elysium, to revel in the pleasures that resort planet offered.

However, Whip Gunther told him that it would be best to cultivate these others, to seemingly become part of their party. Then when they landed, they would go through customs and immigration as though they were a group, and the two of them would be less conspicuous.

Arrival in Elysium couldn't have been simpler. If there were any Interplanpol agents present at the luxurious spaceport, they remained inconspicuously out of the way. The examination of luggage and identification papers was cursory, except that their interplanetary credit cards were checked on a credit screen.

Whip Gunther said dryly, "They want to be sure you have sufficient on hand to be able to afford the pleasures of Elysium." His bandages had been removed, and Venu had been surprised at what the Tangier plastic surgeon had accomplished. Dark red hair was now brown. The broken nose was considerably straighter. The faint scar was gone and the craggy face seemed more full. The color of the eyes had been changed with contact lenses.

There was no difficulty about the interplanetary credit standing. Venu had transferred fifty thousand credits to Whip Gunther's account.

They had gone through the spaceport routine as though they were part of the group of eight Whip Gunther had insisted they chum up to on the *Shepherd*, although that turned out to be a needless precaution. Once through the routine, the adventurer dropped the others without even the bother of saying goodbye. He and Venu took a hovercab into town.

"This is the capital city," he told the younger man, "and the largest one on the planet."

"Where are we going, Sahib Whip? How will we attempt to find Hari Maroon?"

"I know his favorite hotel and casino. I've seen him in the gambling rooms there two or three times. I think he probably owns the place. It's the swankest on Elysium. We can start there. If he's not there, we'll have to think of something else."

"Perhaps he has already left this world."

Whip Gunther shook his head. "I doubt it. I saw his yacht at the spaceport. He seldom travels any other way. At least, so I hear. I'm no authority on the man."

The Baccarat Hotel-Casino was quite the most luxurious establishment Venu Jhabvola had ever marvelled at. It made El Minzah, on Tangier, pale in comparison, and Venu had thought that hostelry quite magnificent. There seemed to be at least two servants for every guest and they were trained to the zenith of perfection.

Three trimly uniformed bellhops and a captain took them to their suite, which was the size of a large apartment and included even an automated kitchen.

When the hotel employees were gone, Whip Gunther put his hands on his hips and whistled silently, appreciatively. "I won-

der what the poor people are doing today,"
he said.

Venu looked about too. "It seems a bit
ostentatious," he said. "Couldn't we have
taken smaller and less expensive accom-
modations?"

"This is the cheapest they had," Whip
Gunther said. He walked to the automated
bar. "Well, we've made it thus far. That
calls for a small amount of celebration."

But even as he began to dial, two men
sauntered in from one of the other rooms.
They were so nearly identical that they could
have been twins. Both were approximately
Whip Gunther's size, both were expressionless of face, both looked very competent.
And both carried guns in their hands.

The first one said, his voice as empty as
his face, "Okay, Gunther, lean up against the
wall with your legs spread." He looked at
Venu. "You too, boy."

"What's the big idea?" Whip Gunther
demanded.

The second of the two gestured with his
pistol. "We've been checked out on you,
Gunther. Get up against the wall for a frisk.
Don't try any of your famous tricks. Our
orders are not to kill you—unless necessary.
But we wouldn't mind. All in a day's work."

Whip Gunther leaned against the wall,
saying, "This is a big mistake. My name's
not Gunther. It's Warren Beattle."

The newcomers didn't even bother to laugh. While one stood alertly to the rear covering, the other thoroughly searched the interplanetary adventurer. He brought forth the laser pistol and dropped it into a side pocket, and then came across the manriki-gusari. He looked at it with mild interest, then dropped it, too, into his pocket.

"Your turn," he said to Venu, who was also leaning against the wall, his legs spread. It was an efficient manner in which to search a person. The position was such that even a man capable of as fast a motion as Whip Gunther could not get into action quickly, certainly not quickly enough to avoid getting shot.

The searcher found Venu's laser pistol.

"Kind of young to be carrying something like this, aren't you?" he said.

Whip Gunther said, "What's all this about?"

"Come along with us," the first one said. "Somebody wants to see you." He motioned with his gun at the door.

They paraded down the hall, the two men with the guns keeping them in their side pockets, but with their hands on them.

At the end of the hall a door opened upon their approach.

"In there," one of them said.

Whip Gunther and Venu entered a large reception room, very efficiently, very luxuriously done. There were three desks. The girls behind them didn't look up at the four newcomers.

Another door, at the far end of the room, opened up.

"In there," the gunman said again.

Whip Gunther and Venu filed through.

The room beyond was a very large office done in the most expensive decor. Behind the largest desk Venu had ever seen was seated a man in his late middle-years, who obviously went to the utmost trouble to keep himself in the best of physical shape. His tanned face was firm. His mustache was so neatly trimmed as to seem artificial.

"Here they are, Mr. Maroon," the first of the gunmen said.

"So I see," the other said. "You two go to the other side of the room and keep your weapons at the ready. This is a very unpredictable man. I am surprised that you had so little difficulty in taking him."

Whip Gunther growled. "The young fellow here was in the field of fire."

The man behind the desk nodded. "I have heard of you, Whip Gunther. At one time I even considered taking you into my service. Unfortunately, when I checked your dossier, I found you had so many, ah, marks against you that it would have taken even me too much trouble to have you cleared. I am, of course, Hari Maroon. Please be seated."

Whip Gunther and Venu took comfortable chairs before the desk.

"How'd you get onto us?" Whip Gunther said, crossing his legs.

"My dear sir. Someone bribed a spaceport official on Medea to reveal my flight plan upon leaving that planet. It was reported back to me. Obviously, I have many enemies. I became curious to find who was interested enough in learning my location that he would pay such an amount. The trail led to our mutual friend, Ahmed Abdallah. A bit of pressure was applied and he revealed that it was the famed Whip Gunther who was responsible not only for delving into my journey from Medea to Tangier, but from Tangier here to Elysium as well. It took very little further checking to find your new identity and the fact that you were en route here on the *Shepherd*. When you applied for reservations in this hotel, I, of course, had you assigned to this floor to make it that much simpler to interview you."

He looked at them questioningly. "So why do you follow me?"

Venu said, "I seek my father," trying to keep trembling from his voice. After all this difficulty, here he was, in the hands of the enemy.

"Your father?" The other touched fingertips to his forehead. Somehow, to Venu, he did not look like a man who could be the most dangerous in the galaxy. "Venu Jhab-vola," he read from the paper before him on the desk. "And from the planet Harappa. You must be the son of Sudhin Jhabvola."

"Yes."

"But why do you think I know anything about your father? I was as amazed as anyone else at his disappearance on Medea."

Venu said, after taking a deep breath, "You are the only one to have profited by his mysterious disappearance . . . or death." It had been difficult to say the last word.

Whip Gunther brought out, "And what about the three attacks on Venu here? One on Medea and two on Tangier. All three were obviously attempts on his life. Only a man like you could have made such arrangements at such distances."

Hari Maroon was absolutely staring at him. "I don't know what you're talking about, man. What attacks?"

Whip Gunther gave the details of the three attempts.

Hari Maroon shook his head. "See here, Gunther, you know my reputation. Now, face reality. If I wished to eliminate this young man, do you think my men would flub the job three times?"

Whip Gunther said gruffly, "I was a bit surprised, myself. It looked like semi-amateur stuff to me."

The interplanetary tycoon looked back at

Venu. "On various occasions I have come up against your father. Business occasions. Sometimes he defeated my interests. However, I both respected and liked him. I realize I have a rather high reputation in some circles, but, I assure you, the only times I resort to physical force is in response to physical force. Large sums of money are usually much more practical."

Venu was feeling dismay. He had based everything on the belief that Hari Maroon was responsible for his father's disappearance, but now he couldn't find it within him to disbelieve the other. He looked at Whip Gunther, who was scowling puzzlement.

Hari Maroon turned to his two bodyguards. "I assume you searched these gentlemen before bringing them into my presence?"

"Yes, sir, of course."

"Return to them whatever you took."

The bodyguard hesitated. "Are you sure, sir? I've checked up on this Whip Gunther, sir."

Hari Maroon looked at him.

The bodyguard said hurriedly, "Yes, sir," and brought the two laser pistols and the manrikigusari from his pockets, came across the room, and grudgingly handed the pistols and chain to Whip Gunther and Venu.

"Put up your own guns," Hari Maroon

said to his two men, without looking at them.

He turned to Venu. "If I was attempting your life, there is nothing to prevent me from doing it now, here in my own establishment, with a hundred of my people on hand to do it and then dispose of your remains. It would be no problem. Even if it was discovered, I would not be embarrassed. The government of this planet is in my pocket."

Whip Gunther's mouth was working. His own laser was in his hand. The bodyguards had holstered theirs as instructed. He put his own gun back into its place, turned, and looked at his younger companion.

"He didn't do it, Venu."

Venu looked at the tycoon in despair. "But, if not you, who?"

Hari Maroon was obviously irritated. "I don't know, confound it. The whole matter makes no sense to me. And I hate things that don't make sense."

Whip Gunther said, "You were on Medea at the time. You must have heard all of the details, especially since you and Venu's father were both trying to wrangle that uranium contract. Can you add anything to the bare facts?"

Hari Maroon shook his head. "I don't believe so. The Medean authorities and the

Harappan Embassy personnel know more about it that I would. But there's one aspect that puzzled me at the time."

Venu said, "What, Sahib Maroon?"

"The way he suddenly disappeared. His communicator and his passport identification were suddenly, simply, not there. Your father was a peaceful man, he was not prone to violence."

"Few of we Harappans are."

"Nevertheless, he was no fool. In his capacity as an expediter for the interests of your planet, he often came in contact with more ruthless men." The other hesitated, then added, "Such as myself."

Venu said, politely, "I do not understand you, sir."

"He was no fool. When confronted with ruthless men who stood in the way of his planet's interests, he was not above defending himself. It was a tight situation, there on Medea. There were half a dozen of us, in all, seeking the uranium rights. He would not be stupid enough to leave himself unguarded, particularly after it was obvious that he had the inside track on getting the contract."

"I do not understand what you are getting at," Venu said, politely but still mystified.

But Whip Gunther said, musingly, "You

mean, whoever got to him must have been somebody he trusted?"

Hari Maroon said, "I can see no other answer. Suppose that your suspicions against me were correct and I was responsible for Sudhin Jhabvola's disappearance, or death. My men would have had first to get through his bodyguard. I assume he had one. But even then he would have had time to shout for assistance through his communicator. And the Medean authorities would have taken an immediate cross on it and come to his assistance. Believe me, on that ultra-efficient, if sterile, planet, the police are unbelievably quick. They would have been there within the minute."

Whip Gunther looked at Venu. "Whom did he trust?"

Venu shook his head in despair.

Hari Maroon said, "Then here is another question. When you first spoke to me you said I was the only one who profited by his disappearance. Now think again. Who else did?"

And Venu Jhabvola's face went empty. He stared, unseeingly, into a far corner of the room.

Whip Gunther said, "What's wrong?"

"I ... I ... know ... where ... my ... father ... is."

"What are you talking about?" Whip Gunther demanded. "Where is he?"

"On Harappa."

Hari Maroon, seemingly always in control of the situation, was flabbergasted. He repeated Whip Gunther's question. "What are you talking about?"

"I ... I can't explain. It is against my religion. If I am wrong, I will have lost merit in this incarnation. However, I am sure my father is on Harappa. I must return there immediately."

Hari Maroon flicked a switch on his desk and said, seemingly into open air, "When is the next spaceship leaving that will touch down on the planet Harappa?"

And as though from emptiness a voice said, "Twenty-eight days from today."

Venu said in horror, "It will be too late."

Hari Maroon touched fingertips to his forehead. He said, "Your father, I understand, is head of the Expediters, uh, subcaste?"

"Yes, yes." Venu was highly distressed. "He is rishi."

"Who becomes head if he dies?"

"I probably do, when I am of age, or immediately, if he is dead of violence."

Hari Maroon flicked his switch again and said, "Order my yacht to be ready for deep space within the hour." He turned and looked at the younger man. "For some time I have been considering expanding my interests into Harappa, the richest gem planet in the Allied Worlds confederation. If your father is still alive, I would like to deal with him. If he is not, this service I render you might lean you in my direction when it comes to negotiations for star sapphires and other stones."

17

Hari Maroon had a luxurious hover limousine at his disposal. The five of them, including the two bodyguards, who sat up in front, rode out to the spaceport in it. When Whip Gunther and Venu put their luggage into the back, Hari Maroon looked at the hamper.

"What in the world is that?" he said.

Venu was embarrassed. "I have been finding difficulty in securing the kind of food which is suitable to my religious beliefs."

"You mean that you're carrying a picnic basket around the galaxy with you?"

"I suppose you might say that."

The other said dryly, as he entered the limousine, "I can only have respect for anyone who will stick that strongly to his beliefs.

In the clutch, most of us only give lip service to the religion we profess."

The driver took them right out to where the interplanetary tycoon's space yacht loomed. It was at least the size of the *Hammerfest 1V* and Venu's mind boggled at the thought of what it must cost to operate it. But then Whip Gunther's words came back to him. Hari Maroon could have bought a couple of worlds if he wanted to.

They left the vehicle and, on Maroon's command, the two bodyguards took the luggage from the car's back compartment and headed for the gangplank. The others followed them.

It was then that three figures detached themselves from the shade the vessel threw. They approached, somewhat warily, and the one in the lead said, "Sorry to disturb you, Mr. Maroon. But this man is the notorious Whip Gunther and we have the duty of putting him under arrest."

Whip Gunther swore under his breath.

Hari Maroon looked indignant. "Confound it, who are you?" he snapped. The two bodyguards had put down the luggage and now stood slightly to one side, legs slightly spread, on the alert.

The newcomer brought forth a wallet and flicked it open to expose the badge inside. "Inspector Roy Donaldson, Interplanetary

Police of Allied Worlds. And these are agents Pol Gruzanski and Helmut Von Hess."

"You've got the wrong man," Whip Gunther growled.

Donaldson shook his head. "Elysium is one of the worlds that criminal elements head for, Gunther. They like to blow their credits when they've just made a score. So we take special efforts here. When you were coming through customs, we photographed the retinas of your eyes. It's even more accurate for identification than fingerprints. The information was flashed back to Earth and the computers in the Hexagon. So it turned out that Warren Beattle is actually Whip Gunther."

Hari Maroon said, snappishly, "What is the charge against this man? He is my guest."

The Interplanpol inspector brought a sheaf of papers from a pocket. "You can just about take your pick. This one on top will do. The planet Orestes wants him as a subversive revolutionist and has these extradition papers out for him."

Whip Gunther said defensively; "It was a democracy until Hans Bohn and his military clique took over. I happened to be there at the time and joined the freedom fighters. They lost. Now Dictator Bohn is in a position to brand all of us subversives and outlaw us. If I'm sent back to Orestes, there won't even be a trial. They'll hang me."

Donaldson shook his head. "That is not the concern of my organization. These extradition papers were cleared."

Venu said suddenly, "An alien cannot take legal action against a citizen of the planet Harappa without the permission of the Gaewar of the province of which he is a citizen. In this case, the Gaewar of the province of New Bombay."

The Interplanpol man looked at him and snorted. "Very fine. But Whip Gunther isn't a citizen of any place, including Harappa."

Venu said stiffly, "His name is Whip Gunther Jhabvola and be belongs to the sub-caste of the Expediters and the Vaishyas caste, into which he has been adopted."

"Nice try, lad, but not good enough. Who adopted him, and when? And where's your evidence?"

"I adopted him, in the name of my father, rishi of the Expediters sub-caste."

"Look, boy," the other said patiently, "we've been checking back on Gunther's recent activities and we've found out that you've evidently hired him to help find your father, who is probably . . . deceased. In which case, how can you adopt him into your family in your father's name, even if that did make sense?"

"If my father is dead, then I am rishi."

For a long moment, all stood there, frustrated.

One of the bodyguards, obviously ready to go into action, said, "Mr. Maroon?"

"Easy," Hari Maroon said. "We seem to be in an impasse, gentlemen." He looked at the Interplanpol men. "I assume you have no desire to antagonize me. Very well. We were about to embark upon my yacht with the intention of going to Harappa to clear up this whole matter. I suggest you come along. Once there you will be able to contact the correct Harappan authorities and see whether what young Venu Jhabvola has just claimed is valid."

It was obvious that Donaldson had no desire to irritate one of the most powerful men in Allied Worlds. However, he was far from happy. He thought about it.

Finally, "Under one condition. Whip Gunther gives me his parole that he doesn't leave the yacht unless his claims are proven. That is, that he is a legal citizen of Harappa and hence by their law cannot be extradited except with the permission of his, uh . . ."

"Gaewar," Venu supplied. "The Gaewar will never give such permission. Sahib Gunther has been performing in the services of Harappa and my people are not ungrateful."

The Interplanpol man looked at Whip Gunther.

"All right," Gunther said. "I give my parole. I will not leave Hari Maroon's yacht until the matter is solved."

The two other agents, who had remained silent during all this, now stepped quickly forward and ran their hands over Whip Gunther's body. One of them came up with his laser pistol.

"Hey," Whip Gunther protested.

"You won't be needing that," Donaldson said.

18

It was decided that Roy Donaldson alone would be sufficient to make the trip. The other two Interplanpol agents would remain on Elysium at their duties. Takeoff was postponed until Donaldson could get his luggage.

The first time Whip Gunther was alone with Venu—they shared a cabin in the yacht—he looked at the younger man quizzically.

"Was that true, what you told Donaldson?"

Venu was ashamed. "No. Only the rishi could adopt you into our family and caste. I could not do it in my father's name. Among other things, I am not even of age. And my uncle is acting rishi. That about the Gaewar is correct, however. Nevertheless, I have lost merit in the eyes of my gods, by telling a falsehood."

Whip Gunther grunted. "Well, the next time I say my prayers, I'll mention you to my gods. Possibly they'll issue you some merit in my behalf. What do you plan to do when we reach Harappa?"

Venu bit his underlip unhappily. "I do not know, Sahib Whip. It will be necessary for me to investigate."

"Well, you'd better figure out something between here and there. Are you sure you can't tell me why you suspect your father is on Harappa?"

"Yes, Sahib Whip. If my suspicions are unworthy I would have lost merit for myself, for my father, through me, and for my caste if I revealed them."

As before, the trip was monotonous. Venu and Whip Gunther spent quite a bit of their time in the seclusion of their cabin, where the older man insisted that the Harappan youth practice with his laser pistol and with the manrikigusari chain.

"Here, try again," he would say. "Now, here is the proper grip. One of the weighted ends is placed in the hand and locked firmly in place with the middle, ring, and little fingers. The chain is then gathered, but shouldn't be knotted or tangled, and placed on top and locked in place by the index finger."

Venu would sigh and try again.

Whip Gunther would say, "Now in the proper circumstances, you can use the chain held like this for brass knucks."

"Brass knucks?"

"Sure, brass knucks. Knuckle-dusters, knucks. Don't you know what brass knucks are?" It was Whip Gunther's turn to sigh. "Venu," he said, "I don't believe you will ever become a, ah, shikari of men."

"But Sahib Whip, by Agni, the sacred fire, I don't wish to."

The trip went smoothly enough. The crew and Maroon's bodyguard kept to their own quarters. Most of the time Hari Maroon spent in his office with two secretaries. Roy Donaldson, Venu, and Whip Gunther would sojourn in the yacht's ample salon, playing battle chess or cards, or watching canned Tri-Di shows. Once the Interplanpol inspector had accepted the situation, there was no animosity between him and Whip Gunther. Indeed, they conducted themselves as though they were old friends.

On one occasion, Whip Gunther said, "What are some of the rest of those warrants you have on me?"

Donaldson brought his sheaf of papers from an inner pocket and read from each of them. When he had completed the lot, Whip Gunther winced.

Donaldson said pleasantly, "I figured it

out in my cabin. If you were found guilty on all of these charges, you would be executed eight times and spend one thousand, two hundred and forty-five years in prison. Two of the executions would be by hanging, four by being shot, one in the electric chair and one in a gas chamber."

Whip Gunther closed his eyes, as though in pain. "I doubt if I could stand it."

Venu was staring at first one of them, then the other. How could men jest about such a matter?

Shortly before they were to set down on Harappa, Hari Maroon had Venu summoned into his office alone and dismissed his secretaries. Venu stood before the other's desk. Maroon eyed him quizzically for a long moment.

Finally, he said, "I have two sons of my own, approximately your age."

"Yes, Sahib Maroon."

"Long since, I've taught myself to detect a fib from a young man. That was a lie you told about being able to adopt Gunther, wasn't it?"

Venu looked at him warily.

The other picked up a desk stylo and tapped its point. "The thing is, as soon as we arrive, Roy Donaldson is going to wish to get in contact with the authorities. When he does, he will find out the truth and arrest Gunther. There would be no escape, since Gunther will be a stranger on a strange world, and conspicuous. Your local police would cooperate with Interplanpol in apprehending him."

"What . . . what can Sahib Whip Gunther and I do?" Venu blurted.

"This uncle of yours, the acting rishi, would he adopt Gunther?"

"I do not think so. I am currently not in favor with him."

"If your father is alive, would he?"

"I think so, since I have given my word."

"This Whip Gunther means quite a bit to you, from what I have seen."

Venu said simply, "Twice he has saved my life, at considerable risk to his own. When I realized the danger to which he was exposed, through me, I offered to release him from his pledge. He refused, although at the time he was convinced that we must fail. At first I did not like him, but now I realize his virtues, in spite of his being a man of violence."

"I see. Very well. How long do you think it would take you to find your father, assuming he is alive? Or to find evidence of his violent death, otherwise?"

"But a few hours at most, in either case."

"Very well. I will make arrangements for us to be held up at quarantine and customs. I will also announce to Mr. Donaldson that our electronic communications system is disabled so that we cannot communicate with the Harappan authorities in regard to Gunther."

"But will he believe you?"

"Probably not, but I can hold him for a few hours. Don't forget, there is but one of him, and thirty in my crew, including my two personal bodyguards. You will have to sneak out of the ship through the cargo hatch. That shouldn't be a difficulty. I've done it myself, in my time."

19

Hari Maroon himself showed Venu Jhabvola the way to the cargo hatch, and as-
sured him that, within minutes of set-down,
it would be open so the Harappan youth
could scurry out. They would land at night,
at a far edge of the spaceport field, and
Venu should be able to make his getaway
before any of the field personnel approached.

It almost happened the way the interplanetary tycoon had planned. But not quite.

As Venu came hurrying down the yacht
corridor, bound for the cargo hatch, he ran
into Whip Gunther, who was leaning non-
chalantly against the bulkhead.

"Where do you think you're going, Sonny?"
he said mildly.

Venu took a deep breath. "I go to seek my father."

"All alone?"

"There is none to go with me."

"There's me."

"But you are forced to remain here in the space yacht. You gave your parole to Sahib Donaldson."

Whip Gunther chuckled. "Venu, my high-minded Harappan friend, how many times, over the years, do you think I've done such things as escape from prison or violate a parole? Offhand, I couldn't count them. I have few principles left. I can't afford them. So let's go. How do we get out of here?"

A voice from behind them said, "That's it, Gunther. Put up your hands!"

Whip Gunther and Venu spun around.

"Sneaky type, aren't you?" Whip Gunther rasped to the Interplanpol inspector who stood there, pistol leveled, a cynical smirk on his face.

Donaldson said, "You forget I've read your complete dossier, Gunther. Your word can be trusted about as far as I could throw you. Now get back to your quarters." He eyed the Harappan youth. "Where do you think you're going?"

"I go to seek my father."

But the inspector had made a mistake in turning his eyes to Venu even for a second.

Whip's hand darted down into his pocket

in a blur, emerged with the manrikigusari, which he whipped out and wrapped around the wrist of the other. Whip Gunther jerked and the inspector stumbled forward toward him, dropping the laser pistol. Whip extended his left hand and straight-armed him. The Interplanpol man collapsed to the deck.

Whip Gunther spun his hand, disentangled the chain, and smashed the strange weapon against the side of the other's head.

Gunther then scooped up the fallen pistol and put it into his clothes. "Let's go," he snapped to the wide-eyed Venu. "When this character comes out of it, there's going to be all hell to pay. As an inspector of Interplanetary Police, he can draw on every cop on this planet to start chasing us."

Venu led the way. Hari Maroon had been true to his word. The cargo hatch was open. They scrambled out of it and down to the tarmac of the spaceport.

"You know the way?" Whip Gunther rasped, as they scurried through the dark.

"Yes. As boys, my friend Attia and I often came out here to moon at the ships from space."

It was a quarter of a mile to the edge of the spaceport. Beyond was a well-travelled highway.

"Now what?" Whip Gunther growled. "The moment we use our interplanetary

176

credit cards in a cab, the computers will have a cross on us."

"But you must realize, Sahib Whip, that I also have a Harappan credit card, issued to me as a student of the New Bombay University. Certainly, it will not be suspect immediately."

"Let's go!"

Venu brought his pocket transceiver out and summoned a hover rickshaw. When it arrived, they climbed in hurriedly. Venu dialed their destination after putting his credit card in the slot for payment deduction.

"Where are we going?" Whip Gunther said.

Venu peered ahead anxiously. "Many years ago there was an evil rajah who dominated the government of the province of New Bombay. He built a large palace, in some respects an evil palace, since it had many secret rooms and even dungeons. After his death, the Expediters sub-caste grew in prominence as Harappa's interplanetary trade became more and more significant. They bought his palace as an administrative center and as a home for the rishi. That is where we go."

"All right." Whip Gunther brought the laser pistol he had appropriated from Roy Donaldson from his pocket and checked its power-pack magazine.

They had entered New Bombay proper

177

and were proceeding down its wide streets. The hover rickshaw stopped.

Venu said, "From here, I think it is best that we go on foot."

"All right, you're the guide. I hope you know what you're doing."

They hurried up the street, finally along a high wall.

Venu said,"The rear of the palace is on the other side of this wall."

Whip Gunther looked up. It was too high to scale. He said, "How do we get over?"

His young companion said uncomfortably, "There is a small gate, but I am afraid that sometimes it is locked. Here it is."

The gate was only about five feet high and was made of very thick wood. Venu tried the heavy iron knob. It was locked. He turned to Whip Gunther in despair.

Whip grunted amusement and brought his laser pistol from his pocket. He said, even as he adjusted the range stud down to five feet, "There wouldn't likely be anyone on the other side, would there?"

"I do not think so, Sahib Whip."

A gleam of ray hissed forth. Whip Gunther made a circular motion of his hand and knob and lock fell out. He cut the beam and pushed the gate open.

"Let's go," he said, still holding the pistol at the ready.

Venu led the way into the dark gardens

beyond. He was obviously completely at home. They approached a massive building.

Venu whispered, "This is a section of the rajah's palace which is no longer utilized. It is very grim and has an air about it of the evil things that once transpired here."

Whip Gunther didn't bother to ask what evil things. He, in his time, had seen a sufficiency of evil.

Venu hesitated for a moment. "I have not been here since I was a young boy. My friend Attia and I used to explore secretly. Had my parents known, they probably would have forbidden us."

He was feeling with his hands along the wall. He stopped and put both palms against what was seemingly a large stone. It gave way inward to reveal a stone staircase leading down. There was no light. Silently, Venu led the way. Whip Gunther put a hand on his shoulder, the better to follow.

"Cloak and dagger stuff," Whip Gunther muttered.

They came to the foot of the stairs and Venu led the way down a stone-paved corridor.

Suddenly a light blazed and a voice grated, "Drop that pistol, or I fire."

The two of them were temporarily blinded. Growling, Whip Gunther let his gun drop. Venu moaned frustration.

For a long moment, the light bathed them.

179

Finally, the voice said, "I did not expect you to come here, Venu Jhabvola."

"I seek my father." And now Venu could recognize the other. He was not overly surprised to see that it was Rana Kumbha, Secretary of the Interplanetary Trade Commission, of the Harappan Embassy on Medea.

The other's dark face mirrored amusement. "Then you have found him, Venu Jhabvola." He motioned with his pistol. "Proceed down the hall. It would seem you know the way. Head for the dungeons. Were you seen entering?"

Venu hesitated before answering, "No."

The other said, "I presume you are the gunman for hire, Whip Gunther. You must make no sudden motions. Believe me, your life hangs by a slim thread. You go ahead. I want the boy between you and me."

Whip Gunther went ahead.

Before long, they began to pass what were obviously dungeon cells. They were dark, the doors closed, but Whip Gunther in his time had seen enough prison cells to recognize them when he saw them. There is a dank odor about the tiny rooms in which man imprisons his fellow man.

They turned a corridor corner and before them was a cell, somewhat larger than the others, from which came artificial light.

Rana Kumbha said, "Stand with your

180

faces to the wall." He brought a key from his pocket.

While they stood as ordered, he activated the lock.

"And now. In there, please."

Venu and Whip Gunther preceded him into the cell. It was possibly twenty feet by thirty feet in extent, and was of stone and windowless. The small peephole in the heavy steel door was the only visual exit to the outside world. The furniture was sparse; a heavy wooden table, a single heavy wooden chair, a steel cot.

Venu put his hands together and said, "Namastey, Father."

Sudhin Jhabvola, who sat at the table, said, "Namastey, my son. And how is it you are here?"

"I came seeking you, my father."

"Of course. You are an honorable son, as I have always known."

"Thank you, Father. The gods function in ways we in this incarnation cannot fathom. However, I am saddened that my efforts have come to naught."

Whip Gunther's palms had become slightly moist. The man with the gun continued to keep Venu between him and Whip. There was no opportunity to snatch out the chain.

Rana Kumbha said, "You two stand against the wall with your faces pressed against it, and your toes touching it."

181

Even as they obeyed him, he took a pocket transceiver from his clothes and said something into it.

Venu said, "Father, it is my pleasure to have the opportunity to reintroduce you to Sahib Whip Gunther, who is again in the services of our family. He has twice saved my unworthy life."

"As he once saved mine," Sudhin Jhabvola said. "My thanks, Whip Gunther. Namastey."

Whip Gunther said tightly, "I'm not doing so well right now. Sorry."

Venu said, "You are well, Father?" He had noted how gaunt Sudhin Jhabvola seemed.

"Within reason, my son. And how is Santha?"

"When last I saw her, she was well, Father, and had taken her position in the household of Uncle Mulk."

Rana Kumbha cut in. "How did you know to come here?"

"It became obvious," Venu said, "after something Hari Maroon said. Sudhin Jhabvola is no fool. During the uranium negotiations he would have been on guard against his rivals or strangers. Only someone quite close to him would have been able to cozen him out of his transceiver and identity papers." He turned slightly from the wall and looked the dark-complexioned trade official in the face. "Only you, on all Medea, fit the description."

Sudhin Jhabvola said, "You are quite correct, my son. He asked to see my things, on the pretext of checking them. And then covered me with a gun and took me to a place of hiding."

Kumbha laughed and ran a thumbnail over his mustache. "Quite a sleuth. And what else did you deduce?"

"Hari Maroon, when he had indicated his own innocence, also asked who else profited by the rishi's disappearance, and at first I could think of none, but then it became obvious."

"Indeed," a new voice said from the doorway.

Venu said, "Yes. The one person in all Allied Worlds who would profit the most by the disappearance of Sudhin Jhabvola was you, Uncle Mulk. For upon such a disappearance you became acting rishi of our family and of the Expediters sub-caste." Venu looked sideways at Whip Gunther. "It is why I could not tell you my suspicions. If they had been unworthy, then I would have lost merit by evilly suspecting my own uncle, and the acting rishi of my family, who ordinarily deserves the greatest of respect and honor."

Mulk Jhabvola entered the cell, his tight face triumphant. "You are a perceptive lad, nephew. However, it is as well that matters have ended in this fashion and that we now have both of our birds in hand. It was proving difficult to eliminate you."

"Yes," Venu said slowly. "You made three attempts. One in my hotel on Medea, which was thwarted by the untimely appearance of two of my fellow guests. Once at the hands of Mohammed ibn Idriss, your hireling in Meknes on Tangier, and once through the two assassins in the home of Ahmed Abdallah. Had it not been for my friend here, Sahib Whip Gunther, you would surely have succeeded."

Mulk Jhabvola looked at Whip Gunther, who still stood there, face to the wall, as ordered, but with his mind racing in an attempt to conceive of a plan of action.

Mulk Jhabvola said distastefully, "So you are the one guilty of upsetting our plans."

There was no need to answer.

Sudhin Jhabvola said, "I have met many men in my work who were ruthless, but never any so utterly so as you, my brother. Your plan was certainly devious. In your position as acting rishi you had available various Expediter spacecraft of all sizes. It was simple enough to send one to Medea, have it land in a desolate area secretly, pick me up, and return me here to Harappa, under guard." He looked at his son. "How did you know it would be here he brought me?"

Venu said, "He would be afraid to land on any other world. The authorities might detect him and all would be exposed. You had to disappear, with no possible way of your body being found, since if it was, I would become rishi. He evidently postponed your death until he was sure that I, too, was eliminated. At first he pretended that he didn't want me to go to Medea, but as soon as I arrived, his man, Rana Kumbha, made quick to reveal to me the presence of the interplanetary credits on Geneva. They wanted me to embark upon my quest for you, knowing that if I was assassinated it would most likely be laid to the door of Hari Maroon."

"Too complicated," Whip Gunther said contemptuously. "Too many wheels that could come off. That's the matter with you characters with twisted minds. You can't do anything simply."

Mulk Jhabvola laughed, his own voice contemptuous. He was obviously enjoying himself. "Indeed? But you see, Whip Gunther, that in the end I have triumphed. We have all three of you. All has been accomplished. And now I am rishi."

Whip Gunther laughed too. Then he shook his head. "There's one thing you've forgotten,

Uncle Mulk. One thing that fouls up your best-laid plans."

Mulk stared at him darkly. "What are you talking about, you fool?"

Sudhin Jhabvola had not become one of the most respected interplanetary expediters through other than ability to read men and situations. He knew Whip Gunther and he was aware of his abnormally fast reactions and reflexes. He knew that Whip Gunther was going to make his play.

So Sudhin Jhabvola chuckled his own humor.

His brother glared at him. "What amuses you?"

Sudhin Jhabvola smiled at him knowingly. "You'll find out, Brother."

Mulk Jhabvola spun about and glared at Whip Gunther. "Turn around. Turn around and face me, you overgrown ape."

Whip Gunther turned, and as he did so, dipped his hand into his side pocket. A beam lashed out from the gun in the hands of Rana Kumbha, but Whip Gunther had thrown himself to the side and then down onto the floor, where he rolled desperately for the far wall, the beam tracing after him across the flagstones.

Whip Gunther, no time to get his chain into action, yelled, "Venu!"

But the call had been unnecessary. The laser pistol had materialized in Venu's hand in a fast draw that would have been worthy of his teacher. The back of Rana Kumbha was to him, as the other attempted to hit Whip Gunther with the laser beam. But now, on hearing the big man call Venu's name, he tried to spin around.

Too late. The laser ray cut entirely through him, went on, and cut through the steel door and on beyond.

Venu was staring wide-eyed as the man crumbled. He directed his eyes down at the gun, unbelievingly.

"Darn it, Sonny," Whip Gunther said, coming to his feet and taking up the fallen man's pistol. "Didn't I tell you to thumb the range stud before using a laser? That ray you just cut loose with has probably burned a hole half way back to the spaceport. You just better hope nobody was in the way."

Venu turned back to his uncle, his face expressionless. "You see, Uncle, you actually did make a mistake, although just now Sahib Whip and father were attempting simply to throw you off guard so that my friend could attack."

Mulk Jhabvola's eyes were popping in fury. "What mistake?" he demanded hoarsely.

"In your attempts to end my present incarnation, you put me in such a position that I changed. When I left Harappa, I was a schoolboy. But in the past few weeks I

187

have seen enough of death and underdealings that I too have become a person of violence. It evidently never occurred to either you or Rana Kumbha that Venu Jhabvola might be armed and know how to handle his weapon."

"Up against the wall, Uncle Mulk," Whip Gunther said with mock sweetness. "I suspect your laws here on Harappa are a bit on the lenient side, and that you might ordinarily survive to try again. So I've got a little present for you that I bought on Tangier, where you can buy anything." He dipped a hand into an inner pocket and came forth with a surette. "It's called Nonvio, and after I've injected you with it, believe me, you're never going to want to do anybody dirty again."

The big man came quickly forward, and before the other could protest, slipped the surette into his arm.

Sudhin Jhabvola had come to his feet, preparatory to embracing his son, but Venu said, "Father, there is one more matter. In our service, Whip Gunther found it necessary to leave the planet Tangier where he had sanctuary. Now he is on the verge of being arrested by the Interplanetary Police on various charges. I have explained to him that if he was a citizen of Harappa he could not be arrested by any alien planet without the permission of the Gaewar."

"I see." The rishi looked at Whip Gunther. "I formally adopt you into the Jhabvola family, into the Expediters sub-caste, and into the Vaishya caste. You are my son, and hence a citizen of the province of New Bombay. I will personally intercede with my friend the Gaewar if any attempt is made to extradite you."

Afterword

Venu was distressed, as they stood making their farewells on the spaceport tarmac. He had grown in the past year. Though his body was still slight, he was almost as tall as Whip Gunther.

"But, my brother," he said. "Why must you go? Here on Harappa, you are safe. If you leave, there are many worlds where your enemies might seek you out, and although Interplanpol may abide by our laws, as they must since we are a member of Allied Worlds, some of the other planets where you have a record might not."

"I imagine I'll wind up going back to Tangier," Whip Gunther said. "Among other things, I have an account to settle with old friend Ahmed Abdallah."

"But why leave? Here you are a respected member of the Expediters."

Whip Gunther grinned ruefully. "I was never cut out to be a trader, Venu. It's your field, not mine. Some day, when you're rishi perhaps, you'll hear through the grapevine or however that old Whip finally came a cropper on one of his romps. I'll will you my manrikigusari. Assuming you have any more characters like your Uncle Mulk around this planet, you could use it."